"On your knees," Leah ordered. Again, the order was carried out with an infuriating slowness. Wendy noticed that the slow actions were totally at odds with the look of love and devotion on the woman's face. She decided to test her theory.

"Don't you think," she said to Leah, "that those two commands were carried out a bit too slowly?"

"I think you're right," Leah said. She caught onto Wendy's plan right away. "Yes, you are right. I think we'll have to do something about that."

Also by
LINDSAY WELSH
Provincetown Summer & Other Stories

BAD HABITS

Lindsay Welsh

A ROSEBUD BOOK

Bad Habits
Copyright © 1992 by Lindsay Welsh
All Rights Reserved

No part of this book may be reproduced, stored in a retrieval system, or transmitted in any form, by any means, including mechanical, electronic, photocopying, recording or otherwise, without prior written permission of the publishers.

First Rosebud Edition 1992

First printing December 1992

ISBN 1-56333-068-7

Cover Photograph © 1992 by Robert Vance Blosser

Published by Masquerade Books, Inc.
801 Second Avenue
New York, N.Y. 10017

ONE

Wendy bent down and deftly fastened the gold buckle on her shoe. The shoes had cost her a small fortune, but they certainly had been worth it. They were impossibly high and the heels ended in stiletto tips, so thin they appeared razor-sharp. The leather had been polished to a high gleam, and the shoes showed off her thin ankles and shapely calves to perfection.

She made a final adjustment to her black costume, then strode purposefully out of the bedroom and walked down the hall. The metal tips on her heels rang out on the gleaming hardwood floor. She knew the sound would be heard through the door.

She stopped for a moment to make a final check in the full-length mirror that hung in the hallway. She liked what she saw. Her long dark hair fell to her shoulders and her makeup was perfect. The black leather corset hugged her body, taut and strong from regular workouts. Her full breasts peeked above the top of the corset, her nipples large and firm. Black panties covered her pussy and black stockings adorned her long legs. One manicured hand held a brown leather riding crop. She smiled with satisfaction and stepped toward the closed door at the end of the hall.

She turned the handle ever so slowly and swung the door open. She caught her breath momentarily at the sight that greeted her, then closed the door behind her and stood so that she could be admired in her stunningly cruel costume.

A young woman knelt in the center of the wooden floor on a small scrap of carpet. Her hands were bound behind her, and a cloth had been wrapped around her head and through her mouth as an effective gag. She was naked save for a pair of tiny white lace panties.

As the leather-clad woman entered the room, the young captive turned her head to look at her. Her blue eyes were wide, filled with a strange mixture of fear and raw sexual anticipation. Her long blonde hair cascaded down the smooth skin of her back.

Wendy smiled. How she loved it when they looked at her like that! She could feel a quick tightening between her legs. She had only known this one for a couple of months and was still trying out a wide range of punishments on her, watching her reactions. Today she had tied her up and left her kneeling on the floor for two hours while she enjoyed a luxurious bath and a good book.

"Well, Brenda, I guess you've been lonely all by yourself," she said. The blonde woman nodded, unable to answer because of the cloth in her mouth.

"I like my slaves to be able to sit quietly when I'm not with them," Wendy continued. She brushed the very tip of the leather crop up her captive's spine. Brenda moaned, muffled by the gag. "You did very well today."

She bent down and released the knot that held the gag in place. Brenda gasped as it dropped away, and gratefully licked her swollen, dry lips. "Thank you, Mistress," she whispered. Wendy could feel her pussy throbbing gently. How she loved to hear them speak so reverently!

She walked slowly around the room, so that Brenda could fully appreciate the stiletto heels, the tight corset, the cruel riding crop. She was slowly turning this spare room into her own private torture chamber. Always on the lookout for unusual and interesting devices, she already had a leather sling hanging from the ceiling and a padded sawhorse fitted with steel rings all over it, perfect for chaining slaves in any position. There were also heavy steel rings screwed into the walls at various heights, from the baseboard right up to the ceiling, which Wendy had installed so that a slave's chains or handcuffs could be snapped to them, forcing her to lie on the floor or stretch out fully against the smooth, hard wall.

For a moment she stopped and caressed the thick brown leather that covered the top of the sawhorse. With satisfaction, she saw Brenda's eyes widen with fear. The young blonde woman had been strapped to the horse a few times, and knew well how tightly it could hold her, and how cruel her mistress could be to her once she was firmly shackled to it. Wendy's long, blood red nails tapped against it; in the silent room, each tap was as loud as a gunshot to Brenda's ears. She visibly relaxed when Wendy moved away from it.

Finally Wendy walked over to Brenda and freed

her wrists from their cruel bonds. Stiffly, Brenda moved her arms.

"Get up," Wendy ordered. Brenda tried, but her poor legs had been cramped for too long on the small square of carpet. She fell on her side.

"Please, Mistress!" she cried out, as Wendy lifted the riding crop. "Please, I'm trying!" But it was no use. The crop left first one welt, then a second on the creamy skin of her back. She cried out as the harsh red marks lifted on her flesh.

"I don't take excuses well," Wendy said coldly, through clenched teeth. "Now, on your feet, or I'll wear this crop out on your hide."

Sobbing, Brenda shakily got to her feet. She swayed a bit, and her legs burned painfully as the cramped muscles responded. But she managed to remain standing.

"I never saw a slave as bad as you are with your excuses," Wendy said. "It seems like every time I give you a command, you find a reason why you can't carry it out. That's a very bad habit, Brenda. I hope you get over it very soon—before I wear my arm out with this crop."

"I'm sorry, Mistress," Brenda said.

Wendy walked over to the sawhorse and again Brenda trembled. But instead of selecting a ring to chain her slave to, Wendy slipped her panties off and sat on the padded top. Her dark pussy was gleaming with her excitement. "Now, slave," she said, "let's see if you can do something right today. Give me some pleasure."

This was a command that Wendy didn't have to repeat, or punctuate with a blow from the riding crop. Brenda truly enjoyed making her mistress come, as often as possible. She rushed over to the sawhorse and bent before Wendy's lovely dark triangle.

deadlines and presentations the way they did, and many of the so-called "business meetings" she attended so frequently were actually luncheon dates with friends or afternoons at the gym. Nothing she did for the company warranted the huge paycheck she received regularly, which allowed her to live the way she so enjoyed.

Nothing, that is, that any other workers knew about. For they had never seen their company's vice-president nude, her hands bound with handcuffs, a ball gag thrust into her mouth, kneeling before Wendy, waiting for the gag to be removed so that she could beg to lick her mistress' dusty leather boots clean with her tongue.

She heard the gentle squeaky "pop" in the kitchen as Brenda opened the bottle of expensive French wine, then heard the cupboard door swing open as she reached for a glass.

She smiled in anticipation, but her lips immediately turned down into a frown as the blonde slave walked into the room.

She jumped up and was on Brenda before the blonde woman even realized what was going on. The object of Wendy's rage was the glass of wine, which Brenda was carrying by the glass rather than the stem, her hand wrapped around it. Wendy slapped her hard and the glass flew out of her hand, smashing against the wall, the precious golden liquid seeping into the thick carpet.

"Idiot!" Wendy hissed, and slapped her again. "Good wine like that, and you treat it like it was rotgut! Don't ever let me catch you carrying wine like that again!"

"Please, Mistress!" Brenda begged. "I'm so sorry, I didn't know!"

Once again, Wendy's hand slapped her cheek,

raising angry red marks on the pale skin. "Don't you talk back to me!" she said. "Now clean up that mess! and bring me another glass of wine—and do it right this time or I'll whip you until you faint!"

Sobbing, Brenda stooped to pick up the remains of the crystal wineglass while Wendy went back to the sofa. She carried the shards into the kitchen, then returned a short while later, with the wineglass on a small silver tray. Brenda presented it to her mistress, still fearful that she wasn't doing it correctly.

Wendy picked it up by the stem. "This is how you handle good wine," she said. "When you carry it by the glass your hand warms it up. Stupid slave, didn't you know that?"

"No, Mistress," Brenda whispered.

"Well, it's about time you learned," Wendy said. "Now clean up the carpet before it stains."

She sipped the chilled wine while Brenda knelt on the carpet, sponging up the spilled liquid. The wine was exquisite, well worth the horrendous price, and Wendy enjoyed it thoroughly. The orgasm and the wine had relaxed her, and she stretched out.

"Slave," she said, "I would like my feet rubbed."

"Right away, Mistress," Brenda said. She hurried to put the sponge back in the kitchen, then knelt by the sofa before her mistress' feet. Wendy admired Brenda's lovely breasts and large nipples as she unbuckled the straps on the leather shoes.

It seemed to Wendy, though, that Brenda was a little clumsy as she removed the shoes. Rather than slipping them off gracefully, she tugged at them and pulled them away from Wendy's feet. She decided to ignore it for the moment, sipping at the wine, but she didn't stay relaxed for very long.

Brenda pushed her thumbs against Wendy's feet, but rather than massaging them firmly, she poked and probed. Finally she pushed Wendy's toes in, and Wendy cried out as her feet cramped painfully.

"Foolish slave!" she hissed. She sat up and dealt Brenda a cruel blow that caught her on the side of the head. Brenda's pained expression was one of a child being punished without knowing the reason.

"Mistress?" she cried. "Mistress, what have I done?"

"You idiot, a massage isn't supposed to hurt!" Wendy hissed. "You're handling my feet like they were hunks of hamburger. Who on earth taught you how to do that?"

"No one, Mistress," she said. "No one ever taught me."

Suddenly it dawned on Wendy just what the problem was. Brenda wasn't being awkward on purpose; she honestly didn't know the proper way to do things.

"You mean to tell me that no one ever sat down with you and taught you how to serve, how to obey?" she asked.

"No, Mistress," Brenda admitted.

For a moment, Wendy almost felt a bit of sympathy for the blonde woman. "So how did you find out what to do?"

"I just picked it up, Mistress," Brenda said. "I did things the way I thought they should be done. If they weren't right, then I got punished, and I knew not to do it that way again."

"I thought you had a couple of mistresses before I met you," Wendy said.

"I did, Mistress," Brenda said. "But they didn't have the nice things you have, and they didn't make me do the things you do. They didn't make me serve them wine or rub their feet, Mistress, so I never knew how it was done."

Wendy drained the glass and put it back on the coffee table. "Well, I'm not about to allow some half-trained slave to tend to me," she said. "Normally I would just throw you out and be done with you—and find another slave who knows what she's doing."

As Wendy paused, Brenda trembled slightly, keeping her eyes on the floor as she knelt beside the sofa. She loved her mistress and the cruel words cut through her like a knife.

"But I think you have a lot of potential," Wendy continued. "You seem to learn quickly, and even if you do some things wrong, I like the fact that you learn from your punishment."

"Thank you, Mistress," Brenda whispered.

"I think you could be a superb slave if only you received the proper training," Wendy said. "I will teach you what you need to know. In return, I ask that you pay attention, watch carefully, and learn perfectly. I will not repeat any lesson twice—for any reason. If I teach you something and you later do it wrong, I *will* find myself a slave who knows what to do. Is that clear?"

"Yes, Mistress!" Brenda said. Her cheeks were flaming; she was thrilled to know that she would be allowed to stay.

Wendy got up, leaving her shoes carelessly cast aside on the leather sofa. "Then we will begin with the basics," she said. "I'm not about to buy new glasses every time I want some wine. Your first lesson will be how to serve me without me having to beat you."

"Yes, Mistress!" Brenda exclaimed, and followed her beloved mistress into the huge kitchen. She knew these lessons would be among the hardest she would ever have to learn, and she was determined to remember them perfectly.

TWO

Wendy looked at her watch, then got up from her desk and walked over to the huge window. Outside, the city was a hive of activity. In the building opposite hers, she could see floors and floors of workers rushing around their offices to get their jobs done. On the sidewalks, people milled about, businessmen with briefcases trying to avoid bicycle couriers. Wendy smiled and stretched luxuriously. The paperwork she'd had to finish for the day was already done and on its way, and she had a luncheon date.

She put on a light jacket, picked up her bag, and walked out of her office. In a smaller office just outside, her secretary was rearranging some files that had already been done earlier that day. Because her boss didn't always generate a lot of paper, quite often she found herself trying to look busy while the rest of the company struggled to make their deadlines each month.

"I have a very important meeting this afternoon, Karen," Wendy told her. "I don't know when I'll be back, or if I'll be back at all. If it goes on too long, I'll just go straight home from there."

"Yes, Ms. Hudson," Karen said.

"If anyone calls for me, tell them I'll call them back tomorrow morning, first thing." She stopped for a moment, and looked at the filing Karen was doing.

Karen dropped her eyes and squirmed in her seat. As much as she liked the leniency of her job, it always bothered her that she did so little to earn her pay. She was always terrified that someone higher up might notice the endless filing and refiling, typing and retyping that she used to fill the hours when there was simply nothing else to do, and fire her.

But Wendy smiled at her, and she immediately relaxed. "It's been pretty slow these last couple of days," Wendy said. "There's no point sitting there doing that."

"Everything else is done, Ms. Hudson," Karen protested.

"I know," Wendy said. She leaned down and spoke quietly lest anyone walking by the office hear her. Karen got a heady, delicious whiff of her perfume. "On my way out, I'll let them know that I need you to take some notes at the meeting. Then lock up and go on home. It's too nice a day to be sitting here, anyway."

Karen's face lit up. "Thank you, Ms. Hudson!" she said, and Wendy smiled again. If only Karen knew how much she loved to hear such words! Her tone was almost the same as that of a slave thanking her mistress for some small favor.

Karen watched as Wendy turned and left the office. Like almost every other employee of the company, she wondered just how Wendy kept her position and her obviously high salary when she appeared to do so very little.

Karen also noticed just how different Wendy was from other people. She was always on top of every situation, and could sway people with almost imperceptible ways that Karen still didn't fully understand. She seemed to take command of any room she walked into, and even when she was being gracious or humorous, there was an iron will behind it that would never bend.

Although she'd worked for Wendy for years, Karen was still in awe of her, and often thought she perceived an open, raw sexuality that was both exciting and a little dangerous. Sometimes she even wondered ... but that was ridiculous, Karen told herself, and she dropped the files into her desk, put her pens away and reached for her coat.

True to her word, Wendy left a message at the front desk in case anyone should question Karen's absence, then waited for the elevator that would take her to the ground floor of the huge office complex. Outside, she hailed a taxi and gave the driver the address of one of the city's better restaurants.

She asked for a secluded table, and received one in a quiet, dark corner. She was a bit early, and ordered a glass of wine while she waited. The service was impeccable, and she watched the waiter's graceful, fluid movements as he set the glass before her. Soon, she thought, such service will be second nature to Brenda.

Brenda! She smiled as she remembered last night. She had often read about the training undertaken by the finest chefs, how they would spend almost a year just washing vegetables and scrubbing pots before they would be allowed to pick up a knife.

She decided that such a process would work for slave training as well. That night, once the last of the spilled wine had been mopped up, Brenda spent an hour at the sink washing every glass in the kitchen, then drying them all and putting them away. She sat with silver polish and a rag until the silver serving trays shone like mirrors. She earned three hard lashes with the riding crop when Wendy discovered a tiny spot of polish left on one of the trays, and had to polish all of them over again.

She was then given the corkscrew, and made to examine it carefully. Wendy let her go through the motions on an empty bottle, explaining the finer points such as cutting the foil collar. But she would not let her work on a corked bottle yet; Wendy wanted the lessons to go slowly and sink in thoroughly. She gave Brenda a slim volume on different types of wine and sent her home, explaining that on her next visit she would be tested on her knowledge.

Wendy looked up and saw Diane being led to her table. As always, her friend looked beautiful. She was dressed in a light suit, which showed her chocolate skin to perfection, and today her hair was pulled back from her face in a sophisticated style. She kissed Wendy's cheek, then slid into the chair opposite her.

"I'm not too late, am I?" she asked, putting her bag down. "There must be some kind of a convention going on by our building—because there's not a taxi to be found!"

"You're not late at all," Wendy replied, then added mischievously, "I don't have to go back anyway."

"Great minds think alike," Diane said. "I told them I'd be out for the rest of the day, too."

They perused the menus given to them, but Wendy couldn't help sneaking glances over the top of hers. Diane was just so beautiful. She, too, was a dominatrix, but she and Wendy were often lovers as well. Wendy knew so well what was under the well-tailored linen suit. So many times she had sucked those delicious dark breasts into her mouth, and touched her hand to the ruby-rich folds of Diane's lovely cunt.

Her own pussy was beginning to throb, and she pressed herself hard into her chair, then reached over and took Diane's hand, caressing it gently before going back to her menu.

When the waiter came back, they ordered three small courses, enough to ensure at least a couple of hours in their secluded spot, plus a bottle of fine French wine.

"So how's your new one working out?" Wendy asked.

"Not too bad, considering how young she is," Diane replied. She had met Alicia through a mutual friend, and had immediately been intrigued with the slightly built, raven-haired beauty. Less than two weeks later, Alicia found herself in Diane's penthouse apartment with a collar around her neck kneeling at Diane's feet—a situation both of them found tremendously exciting.

"She surprised me, though," Diane continued. "She's not very big, you know, and I thought she'd be really frail. But she can take an awful lot. I caught her playing with her pussy one time when I had left her alone and told her to sit still. You know that new rack I bought? I handcuffed her to it and I let her have it good with the lash. She cried a lot, and I had to stuff a gag in her mouth, but she took every bit of it. I was really amazed."

The waiter came back with the bottle of wine, which he presented for their approval, then deftly uncorked it and poured a bit for Wendy to taste. At her nod, he half filled their glasses and left.

"That reminds me of a problem I'm having right now," Wendy said, gesturing to the waiter who had stopped at another table after serving the two women their wine. "I had a big blowup yesterday with Brenda, the little bitch." She recounted the events of the previous day, finishing with the story of the improperly handled wine and the painful massage.

"Doesn't sound good at all," Diane said, sipping her wine.

"You know," Wendy said, "it seems to me that I'm seeing more and more of that type of behavior all the time. I get new ones, and they're just full of bad habits. I know they're young, but they should be able to serve me a glass of wine properly, for heaven's sake. I asked this one who taught her, and she said nobody ever did. I'm not the first mistress she's ever had. Why on earth are women putting up with this kind of behavior?"

"I really don't know," Diane admitted. "I've noticed a lot of bad habits too, but I never really thought about it until you mentioned it just now. I thought maybe I was just being too picky. It seems that almost every one I've had recently has been really rough. You're right, it seems like no one's taking any time to train them properly. They just use them up and send them out to the next person."

Their appetizers arrived, tiny shrimp nestled into perfect avocado halves. The waiter was quite handsome, and Wendy noticed that his eyes never left Diane when he came by the table. Poor fool! she thought to herself. He'd never know that he didn't stand a chance.

"The ones I've met know the actual sexual moves quite well," Wendy said. "I haven't had one yet who was unable to satisfy me. But you know as well as I do that there's a lot more to it than that. I want one who will do what she's told the first time, without any whining about it. I want to be served properly, I want proper massages, I want them to act properly around other mistresses. I don't think that's too much to ask."

"Not at all," Diane agreed. "I think all slaves should be complete ones—and not just for sex. It's very important that they do everything right. How are you going about it with this one?"

"Very slowly," Wendy said. "Actually I have to teach her twice. First I have to train her to get rid of the bad habits, and then I have to teach her the proper ones. She spent the rest of the night washing glasses and polishing the silver. I had to beat her and make her do all the trays over again, but she got the message."

"Sounds good," Diane said huskily. She could picture Wendy standing over her blonde slave, her riding crop falling on the pale skin. Her pussy stirred at the thought.

"I'm going to take everything very slowly with her," Wendy continued. "I want her to learn all the basics first, before I move her onto more advanced things. It's going to take some time, but I'm planning on keeping this one for a while, so I think it'll be a good investment. At least I'll have one that's properly trained, not like the type we keep seeing over and over again."

"Sounds almost like going to school," Diane said.

"A school for slaves," Wendy mused. "Wouldn't it be nice if there was one somewhere? We could send them to be trained and have them come back to us knowing what to do."

"Wendy, you've got it!" Diane exclaimed.

"Got what?"

"A school for slaves!" Diane was very excited by the prospect. "You're doing it the right way, by the sounds of it. Why don't you take on a few pupils and train them all at the same time?"

"Oh, Diane, that sounds like a lot of work," Wendy protested.

"Well, you're not as busy as a lot of us are," Diane said teasingly; she knew exactly how Wendy kept her job. "And admit it, wouldn't you just love to have a whole classroom of slaves obeying your commands and licking your boots?"

"It does sound exciting," Wendy admitted.

"Besides, hon," Diane said, smiling broadly at her little joke, "a girl can always use a little more spending money, can't she?" She also knew how Wendy very handily paid for all of her luxuries.

Wendy still wasn't fully convinced. "But what do I know about running a school?" she asked.

"Well, your little training course that you've got your own slave doing sounds pretty effective," Diane said. "You know what a good slave should be able to do. Come on, who would be better for the job than you?"

Wendy took a deep breath. "All right, I'll do it!" she said. "Will you be my first customer?"

"Done," Diane said. "You let me know when your first class is coming up, and I'll send Alicia over to you. You have carte blanche with her. Do whatever you have to in order to teach her. I don't spare the rod with her, and neither should you."

"I won't," Wendy promised. "That's going to be my first rule: Expect punishment, and plenty of it. I won't let any customer down and return a poorly trained slave to her. Only when I consider a slave perfectly trained to my standards will she be allowed to graduate."

"You always did have pretty high standards," Diane said.

"Well, they're going to go even higher now," Wendy said, and grinned. "I have a business to run!"

The waiter brought their main courses. As Diane had suggested, the thought of a whole classroom of slaves licking her boots was turning Wendy on more and more. Her pussy was throbbing and she looked at Diane longingly.

She could picture them now, hanging onto her every word, trying desperately not to forget a single detail of any lesson. Of course, they wouldn't be able to remember everything, and Wendy would test them on the most difficult items, the most trivial lessons.

She could see two of them falter, their mouths working soundlessly as they tried so hard to find the proper words. She saw their tears and their pleading eyes, begging for mercy and a chance to try again. Of course, there was never a second chance.

She saw her hands grasp the first slave's long hair and throw her to the ground. She could feel the muscles in her arm tighten as she raised the riding crop, bringing it down on the smooth flesh. She saw the cruel welt rise and heard the cry. There was another lash for screaming out. Then she looked over and saw the bloodless cheeks of the second one.

This one, she forced to her hands and knees. Then she grabbed a stiff leather paddle and struck again and again on those tender buttocks until they burned a deep red, and the young woman's face was stained with silent tears. Throwing aside the paddle, she could see herself ordering them both to clean her boots with their tongues. As the two groveled at her feet, she glared a warning to the other students who had answered correctly. In their eyes, she could see two emotions battling for supremacy. One side of them was deathly afraid of doing wrong and undergoing the punishment their mistress so ably handed out. The other side longed for it, and she could see envy in their eyes for the two women whose tongues were gritty from licking her leather shoes. How they longed to lie before their mistress and prove their worth!

"Wendy! Wendy, are you there?" Diane was laughing as Wendy popped out of her fantasy. "You went into another world there."

"I was just thinking about it, and I went right into it," Wendy explained. She certainly had! Her pussy was now burning, and her nipples were hard, aching to be touched. She knew her cheeks were flushed and her whole body was on edge. Her shoulder still felt as tight as if she really had brought the riding crop crashing down on a poor slave's body. The sensation sent a rich thrill through her.

She reached for her wineglass, but it was empty. "Do you want to order another bottle?" she asked.

Diane reached across the table and took her hand. "I have a better idea," she said. "I have a nice bottle chilling at home. Why don't we go there and have a glass?" She had also been thinking about Wendy's school and was just as excited about it as Wendy was.

They motioned the waiter over and canceled their dessert, calling for the check immediately. He watched them as they walked away from their table. They were gorgeous and had been extremely polite to him throughout the meal, but like almost everyone else who came in contact with them, he detected their iron wills, stunning raw sexuality, and also the whiff of danger that seemed to always be around them. To his surprise, he found himself in awe of them and strangely enough, just a little bit jealous of those who understood the danger and who benefitted by it. He didn't understand it himself, but also like most people who met them, he wished he could.

The two women hailed a taxi outside the restaurant for the short trip to Diane's apartment. When they arrived, the doorman helped them out of the car and held the heavy glass door open for them as they walked into the richly furnished lobby. Like Wendy, Diane's taste ran to the expensive, and the well-known address was only part of it.

Her penthouse suite was as luxuriously appointed as Wendy's house. The thick carpet felt delicious under Wendy's feet as she took off her coat and carelessly tossed it on a chair. Then she kicked off her shoes, and sat down on the huge sofa.

Diane went into the kitchen and returned with two crystal glasses of white wine, then sat beside her dark-haired friend and held up her drink in a toast.

"To Wendy's School for Slaves," she said.

"May you be happy with the results," Wendy said, and gently clinked her glass against Diane's before taking a sip. "Even though I only have two pupils."

"I'll take care of that," Diane promised. "I know a few women who have noticed some bad habits in their slaves, too. I'll get in touch with them and see if they'd be interested in your services." She grinned. "We'll quote them an astronomical tuition fee, of course. These women aren't happy unless they're spending lots of money."

She took another sip of her wine, then put the glass down. Taking Wendy's glass from her, she set it down as well, then leaned toward her. "Hon, I can't wait any longer," she said, and put her arm around Wendy's neck, then kissed her deeply.

Wendy returned her kiss immediately, pushing her tongue into Diane's mouth and mingling with hers. Her pussy was throbbing so badly she couldn't stand it any longer. She reached for Diane's firm breasts through the beautiful linen suit.

"Come with me," Diane whispered huskily, and led her to the bedroom that Diane knew so well. The wrought iron, queen-sized bed looked so inviting that she wanted to press Diane onto it and take her right there. But she forced herself to go slowly, to make the afternoon's session last as long as possible.

She felt Diane's hands on the buttons of her shirt as they kissed again. Then her blouse was open, and her large tits were free. Diane massaged them, pinching the nipples. She reached down and took one into her mouth, and Wendy groaned loudly as she felt Diane's hot tongue lash across the hard nub of flesh.

"Let me have you too," she begged, and Diane stood up so that Wendy could unbutton the crisp linen suit. She ran her tongue down Diane's skin with each button she unfastened, until Diane's firm breasts were uncovered. She took each into her hands, sucking on first one nipple and then the other while Diane moaned and arched her back. Then they massaged each other's tits while they kissed.

Wendy reached around and ran her hands over Diane's firm ass, then slowly pulled down the zipper that held her skirt in place. It fell to the floor, revealing a white lace garter belt, black stockings and no panties. Instantly Wendy's hand was on Diane's beautiful dark cunt. She cupped it, enjoying its warmth and moisture, then she slowly slipped her finger between the swollen lips and tickled the ruby clit. Diane moaned and kissed her hard, then insisted that she shed the rest of her clothes too.

She did so happily, and within seconds she was

standing nude, her beautiful furry pussy aching for Diane's touch. Diane, meanwhile, had stretched out on the bed. Her smooth dark skin looked so delicious against the creamy white quilt spread over the bed. "Come here," she begged, and Wendy bent down and kissed her.

Then she was on top of her, her pussy over Diane's mouth, and her own face over Diane's sweet cunt. She could smell the lovely aroma as she bent down and ever so gently whisked the very tip of her tongue over Diane's clit. She felt a quick shiver go through the dark woman as she did.

Then Diane's mouth was on Wendy's clit, and Wendy bent and gave herself over to eating the pussy below her. Her tongue slid between the folds, so steamy hot, and she touched a finger to the entrance of Diane's hole.

Diane grabbed her ass and pulled her down so that she could feast on Wendy's pussy. One fingertip played around Wendy's tightly puckered asshole while her tongue pressed firmly on the wet clit and pushed it back and forth. Both women were groaning loudly, venting the passion they had held back for so long at the restaurant. Wendy wanted to bury her whole face in Diane's cunt and just stay there with her huge clit between her lips.

Diane held Wendy's clit gently between here teeth and used her tongue to snake back and forth across it. Wendy pushed her tongue into Diane's wet hole, pressing in as deeply as possible. She wished her tongue was twice as long.

She could feel Diane speed up, and her clit was on fire as the probing tongue swept back and forth over it. She concentrated on Diane's clit also, and soon they were both moaning loudly and bucking their hips wildly.

Diane came first, crying through her lips, which were closed on Wendy's pussy. She didn't stop her tongue lashing, though, and only a few seconds afterward, Wendy exploded as well. The sweet hot waves went all the way through her, right to her fingertips and toes, and she collapsed in Diane's arms.

"No slave can beat another mistress for sex," Diane gasped. "But I'll be happy if Alicia graduates from your school able to do that even half as well as you do."

"Wouldn't that be nice!" Wendy agreed, and kissed Diane slowly and lovingly. "Well, she'll have standards she'll have to pass. They'll all have to pass my tests before they graduate. Of course," she smiled, "if they don't, they'll just have to take their punishment and learn a few more lessons."

"That sounds even better," Diane said, snuggling close to her bedmate. "Just what kinds of punishment do you have in mind?"

"Well, I already have a sling and a sawhorse," Wendy said. "And a riding crop and a whip, of course. I want to get an X-frame, and some paddles. I'll look around and see what else strikes my fancy, of course."

"Sounds delicious," Diane said, and slowly and almost absently began stroking her own nipples, which quickly turned into hard nubs.

"And a cane!" Wendy exclaimed. "A long, thin cane, for bare bottoms. I've read stories about English boarding schools, and it seemed to me that those beautiful canes were just wasted on those horrible little boys who didn't appreciate them. I want to use one with all the glory it deserves."

"Oh, I love the sound of that one," Diane said. Her hand was now on Wendy's body, stroking her slowly.

"Just imagine them bent over, and their panties

down around their ankles," Wendy said. "That cane would move so fast, it would just be a little whistle in the air. But they'd hear it coming. Think what a perfect, thin little red line it would leave! And I wouldn't stop until that whole ass was crisscrossed with those beautiful red lines."

"Oh, hon, you're going to be a wonderful teacher," Diane whispered. She leaned down and took one of Wendy's hard nipples into her mouth, running her tongue all over it. She cold feel Wendy's fingers exploring her pussy and she moaned and spread her legs wider.

Wendy quickly and expertly slipped down on the bed and positioned herself between Diane's thighs until their pussies were touching. She loved the warm feeling and especially the sight of her creamy white skin and dark pussy hair against Diane's rich, chocolate-colored legs and black mound.

They had done this so many times before that they fell into a rhythm almost immediately. Both of their pussies were still wet and their clits slid over each other, tickled by the wiry pubic hair.

"Oh, hon, rub hard!" Diane begged, and Wendy ground her cunt into Diane's flesh as hard as she could. Their pussies were locked together and they moved their hips quickly, delighting in the hot ripples that went through them each time their clits were massaged.

They were both unbelievably excited at the thought of the caning, and they pressed against each other with an intensity that surprised them. Wendy's whole body seemed to be focused on her steaming pussy as she rubbed on Diane's clit. With each thrust of her hips, she could picture the cane coming down on smooth creamy buttocks. Each time her clit rubbed against Diane's skin she could hear the sharp crack as the whisper-thin, iron-strong cane bit into a slave's flesh.

She came violently, trembling and gasping. As soon as the last wave subsided she sat up and put her hand on Diane's pussy. Her hand was soaked with Diane's nectar almost immediately.

She pushed two fingers into Diane's hole. The velvety-soft muscles held her tightly as her thumb reached up to caress the hot nub of flesh at the top of the delicious ruby pussy. Diane moaned as Wendy rubbed her thumb hard, back and forth across her clit.

"Right there, hon!" Diane moaned. "Just like that, yes!" She was pushing her hips up to meet Wendy's probing fingers. "Oh, you do that so well!"

Finally Wendy kept her thumb on the very tip of Diane's clit, and was rewarded when Diane cried out with the delicious rush of her second orgasm. It was so fervent that her whole body felt it, and Wendy had to wait while she calmed down before they could once again lie in each other's arms.

They snuggled together for a while, until Wendy checked her watch. "It's still early," she said. "I have to do something shopping. Care to go with me?"

"Shopping again?" Diane asked. "Hon, you're going to own so many clothes you'll need another house just to hang them all up."

"Oh, no, no clothes today," Wendy said. "No, different kind of shopping. I need some school supplies."

Diane perked right up. "Well, why didn't you say so?" she said. "Oh course I'd love to go shopping. You'll never hear me say no to an offer like that."

"Then get dressed," Wendy said, getting up from the huge bed. "I've got to get on this right away. School starts very soon and I want to be prepared."

THREE

The doorman held the door open as they came out, then whistled for a cab. He often wondered about this most intriguing resident of the building, and he had his own ideas about what went on between the gorgeous black woman and the different guests who visited her. He knew that there was a world of difference between the women like Wendy, with her confident air and sophistication, and the ones who brushed by him with their eyes on the ground, but he made no connections between them, and couldn't explain why the distinctions were so clear-cut. Diane often thought it would be fun to see his reaction if he ever figured it out; as for Wendy, the door might have been opened by a robot, for all the notice she ever took of him.

The cab dropped them off at their favorite store, nestled between rows of expensive clothing stores in the city's well-heeled district. The windows were filled with the latest leather fashions, all sorts of jackets, dresses and suits, and the front half of the store was filled with racks of buttery-soft leather clothes.

Wendy and Diane ignored these things and walked to the back of the store, the area that made up the bulk of the company's sales. There were no trendy clothes here.

Instead, the walls were lined with an almost unbelievable array of goods. There were leather harnesses and heavy paddles, slings, leather cuffs and grotesque leather and rubber masks, some with zippers to close over the mouth. There were many types of gags, in a variety of materials, and heavy canvas jackets with rings and buckles to render a slave helpless. One wall held different types of whips and riding crops, another handcuffs and collars.

As they stood and admired the display, a woman came out of the back room. Her face brightened as soon as she saw who her customers were.

"Diane! Wendy!" She rushed over and planted a kiss on each cheek. "So good to see you again. What have you been up to?"

"This is a very special shopping trip, Julie," Diane said. "Wendy needs some pretty serious stuff. She's opening up a school."

"A school?" Julie was mystified. "What's this, you're going back to the three Rs?"

"Not quite," Wendy laughed. She explained the circumstances behind it, and Diane's suggestion that she take in students and teach them the proper way to serve their mistresses.

"Sounds like a fantastic idea," Julie said. "I'm surprised no one thought of something like that sooner. I might even know of a few people who could use your services; I'll let you know what they say."

Diane picked up a black braided leather whip, feeling its lovely heft in her hand. "Wendy, you'll need one of these," she said.

"Oh, let's do this properly," Julie said. "There's nothing like a job done right." She picked up a pad and pen. "You'll need a list so that nothing's forgotten. Now, Wendy, do you have enough handcuffs for a whole class?"

An hour and a half later, Wendy and Diane were back out on the sidewalk, each with a shopping bag in her hand. Julie had been very thorough and Wendy felt confident that she had everything she needed to set up an effective "classroom." In addition to a few choice items for her own use, most of the smaller purchases were in her shopping bag; the larger items would be sent to her house later, along with an X-frame Julie had promised to order.

"Are you coming back with me?" Diane asked.

"Oh, I'd love to, but I have to go home," Wendy said. "I want to unpack this stuff before Brenda comes over. I'm testing her on the wine book I gave her to study."

"Then I'll call you later about bringing mine over to you," Diane said, and kissed Wendy's cheek. "Just don't wear yourself out testing this one. I want Alicia to come back to me fully trained."

Diane held her hand out for a taxi, and Wendy watched as she got inside. She waited until the cab turned the corner and disappeared, then she turned and walked back into the store.

Julie was surprised to see her again. "Back so soon? Don't tell me you've tried everything already and you're back for more."

"Not quite," Wendy laughed. "I need your help, and I don't want Diane to know about it. It's going to be my little surprise once the training course is finished."

She explained her plan to Julie, who listened intently with a smile of anticipation on her face, a smile that grew wider the more she heard.

"Oh, Wendy, that's fantastic!" she exclaimed. "Wait a minute." She disappeared into the back room, then returned holding a business card.

"Call this woman," she said. "She's the very best there is. Tell her I sent you."

"I certainly appreciate it, Julie," Wendy said. "And not a word to anyone about it! I want it to be a complete surprise for everyone."

"My lips are sealed," Julie promised. "Oh, I wish I would be there when she does it. Once the word gets around, you're going to be swamped with women bringing their slaves to your school."

"Not so fast, Julie!" Wendy laughed. "I haven't even held my first class yet."

"Well, you'd better enjoy your leisure time while you can," Julie warned. "Once this news travels, you're going to be the busiest schoolteacher around."

"Red or white first?" Wendy demanded.

"A dry white wine precedes a red wine, Mistress," Brenda replied. She shivered a bit, partly because of the cold hardwood floor, mostly because she was terrified that her mistress would trip her up on the information she'd studied.

Once again, she was in the middle of the room, nude but for a cruel device Wendy had purchased that afternoon. The leather restraint held her ankles together, and her wrists were shackled into cuffs attached to it. Her spine was bent over and her smooth creamy back was completely vulnerable to the riding crop Wendy carried in her hand.

"Why do we use different styles of glasses,

slave?" Wendy asked. She was wearing elbow-length leather gloves and occasionally she would slap the riding crop against her palm. The loud smack of leather on leather made Brenda cringe.

"Each style complements the wine it was intended for, Mistress," Brenda said. She stole a quick sideways glance to see if her answer was acceptable, and visibly relaxed when Wendy stepped away from her to prepare a new question. Brenda had studied very hard and was proud of how much she'd remembered, but she also knew that Wendy might twist a question to trap her.

"Was 1934 a good year for port, slave?" The question was rattled off in machine-gun fashion.

"A great vintage, Mistress," Wendy replied, "but not as good as 1931."

Wendy turned her back quickly lest her face reveal her surprise. She knew Brenda had studied hard, but she never dreamed that such information would be retained. She smiled; if Brenda was going to learn all her lessons this well, she was going to make a superb slave.

She turned, and her smile disappeared instantly. Brenda knew she had answered a very difficult question correctly, and her expression was one of pride and satisfaction. She didn't realize that Wendy had seen her or know how angry her mistress had become.

She found out quickly. "Don't be too sure of yourself, slave," Wendy said coldly. "How many bottles make up a rehoboam?"

"Four," Brenda said quickly, then gasped as she realized she had given the wrong answer. "Oh, no, Mistress, six! Six bottles! Forgive me, Mistress, it's six." There were tears in her eyes already.

"A slave who thinks she has outsmarted her mistress does not receive the chance for a second answer," Wendy said quietly. "If it was only the question, I would accept your second answer."

She walked around until she stood in front of Brenda, her stiletto-heeled boots tapping a warning on the polished floor. "But you were so proud of yourself, thinking you were so smart because you got the vintage question right. It was a good answer, slave. But pride is one thing you will never be allowed to have."

The first strike of the crop was so hard Brenda felt her stomach churn, and she swallowed rapidly and blinked back her tears. Wendy felt her pussy tighten as she looked down at the wide red welt she had made on the tender skin. Brenda's back was her canvas, to paint burning red with each stroke.

She brought the crop down twice more, then stood back to admire her work. The three stripes were blood red. "That was for the incorrect answer," she said. "Now there's the matter of your pride."

With her foot she pushed Brenda over. Her wrists and ankles shackled together, Brenda fell helplessly on her side. Through her tears she watched her mistress select a brand-new leather paddle. As Wendy walked back with it, Brenda could see that the paddle's wide face was covered with bright chrome studs.

"No, Mistress, please!" she cried, but of course it did no good. The paddle crashed down on her exposed buttock. With immense satisfaction, Wendy saw that every stud was mirrored in red on her slave's skin. She struck again, drinking in Brenda's cries and pleas for mercy, enjoying the sight of the creamy skin going bloodlessly white for a split second before welling up angry red. She could only strike one buttock, since Brenda was lying on her side, and she compared the untouched flesh with the red skin that she had paddled. Yes, the injured side was so much better!

She punished the slave's ass several more times, then threw the paddle into the corner. Brenda was sobbing, her back and her buttock burning bright red. "I hope this is one lesson you'll learn right away, slave," Wendy hissed. "I will not allow any slave of mine to be proud!"

"I'm sorry, Mistress," Brenda sniffled. "I won't forget, Mistress, I promise!" Her skin was so sore it felt as if it might slip away from her bruised flesh if she moved.

Grasping a think handful of blonde hair, Wendy hauled her helpless slave upright until she was once again sitting on the hard floor. Brenda's mouth opened in pain, but no sound came out.

"Now, slave, I have some news for you," Wendy said, walking about so that her heels tapped on the highly polished floor. Brenda kept her head down, her eyes straight ahead. Her scalp was burning, and her reddened ass and back stung.

"You're not going to be taking your training alone," Wendy continued. At this news, Brenda raised her tear-stained face.

"Mistress?" she asked.

"I'm opening a school for slaves," Wendy explained. "It seems that there are just too many of you out there who are poorly trained. I've decided to take on students and teach them the proper way to serve a mistress."

Brenda's heart sank. Sharing her beloved mistress with other slaves! A sob escaped her lips.

"What's wrong, slave?" Wendy demanded.

"Oh, Mistress," Brenda cried, "I love you so

much, and it hurts me to think of other slaves trying to get your attention!"

Wendy stood in front of her and leaned down, taking Brenda's chin between her well-manicured fingers and lifting it. "Very touching, slave," she murmured. "Very touching indeed."

Then, so swiftly that Brenda didn't even see it coming, she smacked the helpless slave's cheek with a ferocious backhand. Once again Brenda fell to her side on the hard floor. The blow, delivered from a gloved hand, burned brightly on Brenda's pale cheek.

"I told you what I was going to do," Wendy said coldly. "I didn't ask for your opinion on it."

"I'm so sorry, Mistress!" Brenda sobbed. There didn't seem to be a single part of her body that didn't hurt. She wanted desperately to wipe away her tears and put a comforting hand to her cheek, but her wrists were secured to her ankles by the heavy leather restraints.

Wendy continued as calmly as if nothing had happened. "My holding the classes here will mean some extra responsibility on your part," she said.

"Yes, Mistress," Brenda whispered.

"The mistresses who are sending their slaves to me are doing so because they believe I am the best person to train them," Wendy said. "Now, how would it look if my own slave wasn't obedient?"

When Brenda didn't answer right away, she felt the sharp toe of Wendy's boot connect with her thigh. "Not very good, Mistress!" she said.

"It wouldn't look good at all," Wendy concurred. "Now, these mistresses understand that you're still undergoing training as well. It will be understood if you are still ignorant about a few things that we haven't covered in class yet."

She picked up the riding crop and brushed

Brenda's spine with it. Shackled and helpless, Brenda held her breath, fearful that the whip would land. "What won't be understood is if you don't listen in class. If you misbehave. If you answer back rudely, or if you don't reply when you're spoken to. Is that understood?"

"Yes, Mistress," Brenda whispered.

"I will be relying on you to set an example for the other slaves in class," Wendy said. "Your manners will be beyond reproach. You will learn your lessons thoroughly, and we'll have none of this pride that you flaunted before me earlier. You will be a model student in every respect. Is this understood?"

"Yes, Mistress," Brenda said.

"Good. I'm glad we agree on that," Wendy said coldly. "Because your options are very plain. You can behave as you should, or I can find myself another personal slave. It doesn't matter to me."

Brenda felt numb. She knew that Wendy meant exactly what she said, and that she could very easily find herself without a mistress.

"Is it very plain to you?" Wendy demanded.

"Oh, yes, Mistress!" Brenda whispered.

"Very good," Wendy said, and turned on her heel. "The first official class begins tomorrow." She left the room, closing the door firmly behind her. Brenda remained on her side on the floor, her hands and feet shackled together, her whole body aching. She didn't know if she would be left like this for a few minutes or several hours. She began to concentrate on each individual pain, on her battered ass, her back crisscrossed by whip marks, her cheek bruised by her mistress' leather glove—and her pussy tightened and throbbed at the thought of each one.

FOUR

"Good morning, class," Wendy said, closing the door behind her.

"Good morning, Mistress," three voices chimed together.

Wendy smiled her approval. The three were kneeling on the floor in a row, their hands held behind them by the handcuffs she had snapped onto their wrists before ordering them into the classroom. They were naked, except for the collars she had decided upon for all of her students. These were heavy black leather dog collars, complete with chrome rings, which hung loosely around their throats. A leash could be applied easily or, if necessary, she could wrap her whole fist around the collar to drag a slave around by it.

First in the row was her own Brenda, her eyes

firmly on the floor, very unhappy about sharing her mistress, but too wise now to let it show.

Beside her was Diane's slave, Alicia, the youngest of the three. She was thin and fragile looking, and her beautiful hair was a heavy black crown. But Wendy had received a full description from Diane, and knew that Alicia could take whatever punishment was necessary to bring her in line.

The third slave was Leslie, who belonged to Diane's friend Anne. She was obviously uncomfortable on the hard floor, and was fidgeting with her shackled wrists; Wendy guessed that she hadn't been a slave for very long. Her brown hair was cut short and threads of silver were just starting to weave through it. She was slightly plump, with large delicious breasts and a dark triangle between her legs. Wendy had only met Anne once, when Diane brought her over to introduce them and enroll Leslie in the school. She knew nothing about this new slave and looked forward to the challenge.

Her "classroom" was done to her taste as well. The walls still smelled faintly of fresh paint, and the hardwood floor had been buffed to a high shine—by Brenda, nude and on her hands and knees. On one wall was a large, school-type chalkboard. It looked extremely out of place against the adjoining wall, which was dotted with hooks. The hooks were filled with the tools of the school's trade: whips, crops, masks, handcuffs, leather shackles, leashes, a straitjacket, paddles, and Wendy's prized cane.

The sling still hung from the ceiling, and the padded sawhorse was pushed against one wall. But there was another toy: a wooden X-frame, with rings at each end, its arms spread wide to stretch out a disobedient slave.

Leslie had obviously never seen so many devices

in one room before, and she kept looking around the room. Brenda and Alicia looked at the floor, but all three of them sprang to attention when Wendy announced that school was now in session.

Their teacher was certainly dressed for the occasion. Wendy was wearing a tight black lace corset, with fishnet stockings snapped into the garters. Her open-fingered gloves were made of matching black lace and reached to her elbows. The corset covered her beautiful breasts, but her dark cunt was exposed and she knew that the three slaves were eyeing it. Her feet were clad in her favorite stiletto-heeled leather boots.

"I am Mistress Wendy, your teacher," she announced. "Your class is now in session, and I will begin with some rules.

"My number-one rule is that you are to remember that I am training you on behalf of your mistress, who has given me permission to treat you as if you were my own. You cannot expect any leniency from me, none whatsoever. I am not the type of mistress who thinks about what she would like to do to a disobedient slave. I do it."

She walked over to Brenda, who kept her eyes on the floor. "Turn your head, slave," she said. The other two immediately noticed Brenda's bruised and swollen cheek, the result of Wendy's leather-gloved blow. "Now look at her back," Wendy ordered, and they noticed the puffiness that remained from the lashes with the riding crop and the leather paddle.

"This is what you can expect," Wendy said. "No slaps on the wrist here. You will learn, and if I have to beat your lessons into you, then that's the way I'll do it." Again she saw the confused look in the women's eyes; half fearful, half longing for the punishment.

"I will be teaching you everything you need to

know about being a slave," Wendy continued. "We will learn such things as how to pleasure a mistress properly, and how to serve her food and wine correctly. We will learn proper manners, and how to behave when her friends are around."

She paced in front of them slowly. Brenda and Alicia watched the ground, while Leslie still stole curious glances around her. "At the end of your training course, I will assess each one of you and decide if you are good enough to graduate. If you are not, you will continue your lessons until you are."

She stopped and smiled at them. "I think you will all want to graduate the first time. There is a very special surprise waiting for those slaves who do graduate from this school, and I don't think you'll want to miss it. It will be something that will differentiate you from ordinary slaves and will show that you have been specially trained to properly serve your mistress superbly. If I were you, I would make every effort to earn it."

She paced again, then stopped before Leslie, her delicious dark pussy right before the bound slave's face. "Service me," she said.

Leslie looked up at her, questioningly. "Mistress?"

Wendy cracked her hard across her cheek with the back of her hand; Leslie's head snapped sideways and her skin burned red. Wendy's voice was quiet and icy. "I know that you are new to this," she said, "so I will teach you your lesson now. When a mistress gives you an order, no matter what it is, you do not question it. Ever. You do what you are told the first time, right away. Is that understood?"

"Yes, Mistress," Leslie whispered. Both her cheeks were burning now, from the blow and from her shame.

Once again, Wendy positioned herself before Leslie's face. "Service me."

This time there were no questions. Leslie pushed the tip of her tongue into the folds of Wendy's dark pussy, at first timidly, then a little bolder. "You two may watch this," Wendy told Brenda and Alicia. "Then we can discuss it."

The room was silent except for the sound of Leslie's lapping tongue. She tried eagerly, but out of the corner of her eye, Wendy could see Brenda almost imperceptibly shake her head with disapproval. The young blonde submissive knew most of the motions that her mistress liked best, and it seemed that Leslie wasn't even coming close.

Wendy stood for fifteen minutes while Leslie licked and sucked at this most sensitive part of her body. Her expression never changed from a look of boredom. Leslie had never been called on to perform this duty for so long, and her tongue was sore and her jaw cramped. But the rich smell of Wendy's pussy, and the excitement of licking this cruel and unforgiving Mistress overshadowed her discomfort. She licked and sucked eagerly, and since she didn't dare look up into Wendy's eyes, she thought her clumsy movements were pleasing the woman whose cunt had been thrust before her mouth. Her own pussy was throbbing and she longed to touch her cunt lips for relief, but of course he hands were firmly held by the cold steel cuffs.

Finally, completely bored, Wendy stepped back. Leslie licked her glistening lips, savoring a last taste of the delicious pussy she had just enjoyed. But her eyes flew open in horror when she heard Wendy's quiet, steely voice.

"You are a most useless slut," she said. "I can see why your mistress sent you to me. I think I would rather go without than have you service me. You are sloppy and clumsy; I can see where a lot of your training will have to lie."

Tears appeared at the corners of Leslie's eyes. "You are fortunate that this is only an assessment," Wendy continued. "If any slave of mine performed like that, I would horsewhip her."

She walked behind Leslie and gently caressed the back of her neck. Her touch was like ice to the submissive, who shivered in fear. "We will work on it," Wendy said. "Right now you are worthless scum, but with time and lessons, I will make you superb. All of you will be, because no matter how long it takes, no slave will leave my school until she is perfect, and until she carries the proof that she has graduated. I will accept nothing less."

She walked around, her razor-sharp heels tapping on the floor, and stood before Alicia. "Let's see what you can do," she said, and thrust her dark triangle into the face of Diane's slave.

Alicia was determined to outshine Leslie. Unable to use her hands, she probed with her tongue between the folds of Wendy's pussy until she reached the clit. She played with it for a while, running her tongue along both sides of it, then she flicked her tongue straight across it. She grasped it gently between her teeth and tickled it with the tip of her tongue, then sucked it in between her lips. She was rewarded with Wendy's sweet nectar, which she hungrily lapped up. Wendy's expression still did not change. This slave was much better than the first, but still desperately in need of lessons.

Alicia was becoming more turned on each moment and, like Leslie, she longed to be able to touch herself for relief. Of course she knew that it would not have been allowed, even without the handcuffs, and her pussy throbbed uncontrollably all the time her tongue was buried in Mistress Wendy's sweet bush.

She wanted to push her tongue right into Wendy's tight hole, but could not lean forward far enough. Instead, she played her tongue across its opening as best she could before returning to Wendy's beautiful clit. It was heavenly to suck on it, and she was bitterly disappointed when Wendy finally stepped back from her.

"Your mistress described you very well," Wendy said. "She told me that your skills were barely adequate. She was right. You will need considerably more training before I decide that you are good enough to pass my test."

Now she stood before her own slave, who was waiting eagerly for her turn at Wendy's pussy. She was proud of herself, for she knew that her skills were so much better than those of the women bound beside her. She had learned her lesson thoroughly, though, and not a trace of it showed on her face, which was still bruised from her previous error.

Wordlessly, Wendy stood in front of Brenda with her legs apart. Brenda was on her clit in an instant. Wendy's face betrayed no emotion, but she thoroughly enjoyed the warm rush from her pussy as Brenda's tongue made its contact.

She knew full well that Brenda's performance was not only based on a desire to please her mistress, but to point out the difference between herself and the other two slaves. Wendy didn't particularly care. At that moment, the hot tongue on her cunt was of prime importance even if she didn't let it show.

Brenda worked her clit the way she knew her mistress liked. Wendy's hot juice was quickly lapped up as Brenda licked both sides of the hard nub, then concentrated on the very tip of it. First she teased it lightly, then pushed hard against it, her tongue flicking quickly back and forth. Wendy's whole pussy was hot and throbbing, and she could feel the sweet buildup beginning in her belly.

Brenda knew the effect her tongue was having, and she stepped up her efforts. Her tongue was now flashing over Wendy's clit and teasing the entrance to her velvety hole. As always, Wendy's expression never changed, but she shivered slightly as the sweet, delicious hot waves rushed all through her body when she came. She stepped away, her dark pussy hair glistening from Brenda's mouth and her own rich juice.

"As you can see, this slave is much better at servicing a mistress than you are," Wendy told the other two. "She still needs much fine-tuning, and will be learning her lessons the same way you will be. But I expect both of you, within the week, to be at the point where she is now. If you aren't, I shall be very disappointed, and I'm sure you don't want that to happen."

Wendy picked up the small key and walked behind her three charges, unsnapping their handcuffs. Each woman stretched her arms out, trying to work the muscles out of their cruel positions.

"Now that I have assessed you, it's time to start your training in this most vital area," she said, and left the room. When she returned, she carried three halves of green pepper, the central rib still intact.

"At this stage, these will be your workbooks," she said, handing each woman one of the pieces. "I expect that when you go home, you will use similar ones for your homework. I don't want to feel your tongues on me again until you are qualified enough to do so. I can't be bothered spending my time standing here, while you worthless scum attempt to lick my cunt. I'll wait until you're good enough to at least raise my interest a little bit."

The three slaves looked at the vegetable halves they had been given, a bit puzzled. Leslie ran her hand over the smooth green skin.

"Stupid slaves," Wendy muttered. She roughly took the pepper away from Leslie and handed it back to her with the cut side up, then shoved the woman's hand to her face. "Imagine that this pepper is my cunt," she said. "Now lick it like it's supposed to be licked. Like you'll be punished if you don't do it right. Which you will," she added threateningly.

Indeed, the hard green pepper shell surrounding the thick white central rib did like a lot like a pussy, once it was pointed out to them. Brenda, determined to show the other two up, ran her tongue lightly around the shell and teased the rib with the very tip of her tongue. The other two women pushed at the rib with the flat of their tongues.

Wendy had had enough. Picking up the riding crop, she slashed Leslie hard across her smooth back. None of them knew the blow was coming, and the sharp smack of leather on skin made them jump. Leslie cried out as a vicious red welt rose up on her skin. "Please, Mistress!" she cried out. Wendy responded with a second cruel blow. Leslie sobbed.

"You are to speak only when spoken to," Wendy hissed. "That was what the second blow was for. The first was for not learning your original lesson. When I assessed you, I informed you that your performance was worthless. I see that, given a second chance, you have done nothing to improve it. I do not expect perfection immediately, but I do expect that you will learn something with each criticism you are given and that you will do better each time. Do you understand?"

"Yes, Mistress," Leslie said, sniffling. Quickly she retrieved the pepper lest she be punished for dropping it. Her back was on fire and her face burned with shame. The other two women glanced at her, fearful that their mistress' rage wasn't completely vented and that they could be next.

"Brenda, lick your pepper," Wendy ordered, and Brenda quickly brought the vegetable to her mouth. She continued as before, slowly running up and down the shell as if she were probing the outer lips of her mistress' sweet pussy. She slipped her tongue inside it as she did when she parted Wendy's pussy lips with the very tip of her tongue. She played with the bottom of the pepper, pretending that it was the entrance to her mistress' tight hole, then slowly and teasingly worked her way up the central rib until she reached the spot where her mistress' clit would be waiting, eager to be flicked and sucked. She lavished attention on this spot as the other two women watched.

"You can see the obvious difference between what you did and what she is doing now," Wendy continued, pacing back and forth as Alicia and Leslie watched Brenda passionately licking the pepper. "You all have pussies, don't you? You know which areas are sensitive, don't you? So pay attention to those places where your tongue will do the most good!"

Brenda's tongue was now flicking madly across the top of the pepper. Her own pussy was hot, imagining that once again her tongue was buried in Wendy's crotch. She loved her mistress and especially loved it when she was given the privilege of licking her. She was determined that her work would ensure another session at her mistress' feet.

"Note how she moves her tongue across the

top," Wendy coached the other two. "That is how you should be treating the clitoris. But she doesn't stay there too long, because she wants to give equal time to the other areas. Now she's going all around the outside. That's how your tongues should be pressing against the pussy lips just before you move inside." The two slaves watched as Brenda continued to run her tongue over the pepper.

"Now, let's see you two do it," Wendy ordered. The crop was still in her hand, and Leslie's eyes stayed on it as she raised the pepper to her lips.

There was a marked improvement in both of them. This time they paid special attention to the shell before zeroing in on the rib that symbolized the clit. "Much better," Wendy crooned as she watched all three licking and sucking as eagerly as if their mouths were pleasing her own pussy. "See, it isn't difficult. You just have to pay attention and try harder."

She walked behind them and stood while they licked the peppers. She knew that each one was on edge, trying her best to please her, since they had no idea if or when a blow was coming. She was thrilled to see that their movements were becoming easier and more fluid as she watched. Just that small improvement let her know that her school was going to be a success.

Ten minutes later she gave the order to relax. She collected the peppers, then stood before them. The three slaves had been kneeling on the hard floor for some time, and Wendy noticed with growing disgust that Alicia and Leslie were not sitting up straight.

Roughly, she grabbed hold of the leather collar around Leslie's throat and yanked her upright with it. "No slave will ever graduate if she doesn't learn proper posture," Wendy hissed. Terrified, Leslie remained straight once the hand was off her collar.

Wendy moved so quickly that Alicia was still off guard when her collar was grasped. Wendy's hand grasped a large lock of hair along with the collar, and Alicia's head was roughly pulled back. "Mistress, that hurts!" she protested.

Scarcely believing her ears, Wendy let go and stepped back. "What did you say?" she demanded.

Realizing what she had done, Alicia clapped her hand over her mouth, but it was too late. "What did you say, scum?" Wendy insisted again.

"Nothing—nothing, Mistress," Alicia replied, her voice trembling with fear.

Brenda and Leslie looked straight ahead, not daring to glance over, as Wendy moved back to glare at Alicia. Her voice was low and icy. "This is not some freethinking college," she said. "This is a school for slaves. For students who do not comment on the things their teacher does. And especially, for students who do not lie to their teachers when they are asked a question."

She stood before Alicia, who was trembling. "Stand up," she ordered. Alicia did so immediately. "Over to the horse."

Teacher and student walked over to the padded sawhorse standing against the wall. Deftly, Wendy snapped a pair of handcuffs on each wrist, then bent Alicia over the horse and attached the cuffs to rings on the sawhorse legs. Alicia's bare ass was now at Wendy's mercy, and Wendy could see that her dark pussy was glistening with excitement even as she trembled with fear.

Wendy picked up one of the discarded pepper halves, and pulled Alicia's head up by her hair, then roughly shoved the pepper into her mouth as a gag.

"You two turn around and watch this," Wendy ordered Brenda and Leslie. "I want you to see exactly what will happen if I am not implicitly obeyed."

She went over to the wall containing her gruesome collection of toys, and deliberated for some time. Out of the corner of her eye, she could see Alicia watching her. She touched the studded leather paddle and noted with satisfaction how Alicia's eyes widened. She teased the bound slave several times like this, caressing a heavy plaited leather whip and a heavy leather belt. Finally she reached for her boarding-school cane.

She had never used it before, and she whipped it back and forth a few times in the air. It was supple and the end flexed back and forth. There was a low whistle of rushing air as she moved it around. She smiled; she had really been looking forward to trying it out.

Back at the sawhorse, she decided to make the most of this lesson. First she gently rubbed her fingers over Alicia's creamy, smooth ass. Then she ran the cane over her skin with whisper-light strokes. Alicia moaned, her cries muffled by the pepper in her mouth.

Then Wendy turned the cane around, and used the handle to rub on Alicia's glistening pussy. The black-haired slave groaned with delight, and pushed her pussy against the cane. Wendy knew it would feel so delicious on those starved cunt lips. She rubbed until Alicia's moans got louder, and then abruptly pulled the cane away. Alicia slumped in frustration.

She tensed up again, though, when she realized that Wendy was getting ready to strike. Wendy noticed the muscles in her asscheeks tighten as she raised the cruel thin cane.

The cane made a thin whistling sound as Wendy

brought it down. It landed with a loud, satisfying crack on Alicia's bare buttocks. She jumped, but the cold steel handcuffs held her firmly across the sawhorse. The pepper muffled her cry of pain.

Wendy stepped closer to see the effect of the cane. A red line, as delicate as a ruby pinstripe, rose up on the white skin. Wendy shivered with excitement and traced the line with one long fingernail. The welt matched the blood red enamel on her nail.

Again she raised the cane, and again the whistling, the sharp crack. This line overlapped the first. In quick succession, Wendy brought the cane down several more times, until Alicia's burning ass was bright red and covered with thin welts. Tears were streaming down her cheeks and only the pepper in her mouth prevented her from screaming in agony.

"Come over here," Wendy ordered, and Brenda and Leslie got up stiffly and walked over. "Look carefully." The two examined the thin red stripes on Alicia's bare ass, once again with that mixture of terror and longing. "I will not stand for any bad habits in my students. You cannot graduate with bad habits, and you will be punished for them. Let this be a lesson to you."

She ordered them back to their positions on the hard floor, then unlocked the handcuffs on Alicia's wrists. The black-haired slave stood up and removed the pepper from her mouth as ordered. Her face was flushed bright red and her eyes were rimmed with tears. To prolong the agony, Wendy forced her to sit on her ass while the other two knelt. The wooden floor was no comfort to her burning caned buttocks.

Wendy picked up a piece of chalk and stepped over to the blackboard. In her fine hand, she wrote the heading "Dinner Settings," then turned to the three naked women, their slave collars about their throats, and smiled.

"There's much more to being a slave than being able to lick peppers," she said. "Who can tell me which side the forks go on?"

Three hands shot up, and Wendy smiled again. They had come to her with bad habits, but Wendy was sure that they would graduate as superb examples of the dominatrix's art.

FIVE

The stunningly dressed dark-haired woman set her drink back down on the table and leaned forward. "I was just so thrilled when I heard that you were running this school, Wendy," she said. "I knew you were the answer to my prayers. I just hope you know what you're getting into by accepting this one."

Wendy took a sip of her own drink. "I think I can handle it, Leah," she smiled. "I'm determined that no one will ever drop out of my school. No matter how long it takes, every slave will graduate."

She sat back and looked around the room for the waiter. The two women were sitting in the lounge of an opulent downtown hotel, Wendy having informed the other managers in her office that she had an important meeting with a client.

That was true, but certainly not the way they would ever have dreamed. Leah was another one of

Wendy's occasional lovers. She had heard about the school and invited the teacher out to discuss putting two of her slaves through training.

"Ellen's been with me for a couple of months now, and she really isn't much of a problem," Leah continued. "She's rough, and I'd like you to smooth her out and teach her some of the finer arts."

"That's no problem," Wendy replied. She had seen Ellen a couple of times; she was a very small woman with beautiful full breasts and creamy skin that took a lash so well. Wendy had only seen her naked, wearing wrist cuffs. It was delicious to think of having the small, fine woman under her control.

"Margot's the problem one," Leah said. "I'm still very confused about her, and I'd like your opinion before I even bother enrolling her in your class. I've known her for only a few weeks, and I don't know if she's worth the trouble."

"Why not?" Wendy asked.

"Well, she's got the strangest attitude I've ever seen in a slave," Leah said. "At first, I wasn't even sure if she was one. She fights me all the way. She won't do what she's told no matter how she's threatened; sometimes it seems like she's the mistress!"

"She wants punishment," Wendy observed.

"I suspected that, but she fights the punishment too," Leah said. "I even sat down with her and asked if this was what she wanted, and she said yes. But no sooner had she said that, then she got that wicked look in her eye again and wouldn't obey me at all."

"What kind of punishment did you use?" Wendy asked.

"The standard type, I guess," Leah said. "I tried a riding crop and a whip, but nothing more exotic than that."

Wendy smiled, a cruel smile that Leah found

very enticing. Wendy could feel her pussy getting wet at the thought. "I think that with some real punishment, you could have one of the best slaves around," she said.

"Do you really think so?" Leah took another sip of her drink.

"I really do," Wendy said. "Think of a racehorse. It doesn't want that saddle on its back and it fights, but the trainer wins out and the horse has to wear it. That horse doesn't want to carry the jockey, and he doesn't want the bit in his mouth, but they're forced on him. Then they put him in the starting gate. He's furious because he doesn't want all these things on him. Then they open that gate and he runs faster than any other horse around, because he's got all that pent-up emotion in him."

She reached over and touched Leah's hand. "It sounds to me like you have a racehorse on your hands. It's going to be difficult to keep her in line, but once we do, she'll outperform any of the others because it's all inside her. She needs some serious humiliation and some drastic punishment. We need to get all of that emotion under control so we can put it to good use."

The sound of her own words was turning Wendy on. In her mind's eye, she was looking over her wall of instruments, deciding which ones were severe enough for a challenge such as this. She could picture Margot spread-eagled, firmly fastened to the X-frame, or at her mercy hanging from the leather sling on the ceiling. She looked over at Leah and smiled, and the sultry look that Leah returned made her clit throb with desire. Leah's lips were sweet and full, and Wendy longed to reach over the table and kiss them.

"So long as you don't think it's too much of a challenge, I'll send them both over to you," Leah said.

"I just know I'm right about this one," Wendy said. "In fact, I'll make a deal with you to prove how sure I am. You pay the tuition for the other one—Ellen, is it? You don't pay me anything for this tough one until she's graduated from school. If I can't make her toe the line, then you don't owe me anything for any of the lessons that I give her."

"Fair enough," Leah said. "I really do hope you can turn her into a real slave, though. I don't know why, but I find her really exciting even if she is difficult to control. Maybe it's like you said; maybe it's all that pent-up emotion in her. Perhaps it just needs to be harnessed."

"I'll harness it for sure," Wendy said, and she shivered just a little as a hot rush went through her from her pussy. She could almost feel the heavy braided whip in her hand, ready to land it on a smooth back. She had had many clumsy slaves and several novices, but never before an unwilling slave who still wanted to be a slave. Strangely enough, she found herself looking forward to having this new student in her class.

"I suppose you have a contract or something that you want me to sign," Leah said. "I'd like to get them enrolled right away."

"No, no contracts," Wendy said. "Just let me know when they can begin."

"Nothing to sign?" Leah asked. She feigned a look of disappointment. "I was hoping you'd have to come back to my apartment to have me fill out the forms."

Wendy smiled. She could feel her panties growing damp as she admired her friend. "Maybe in lieu of forms, we can just get together and discuss what I'll be putting your slaves through," she said. By the look in Leah's eyes, she could see that the dark-haired beauty was just as turned on as she was.

Leah paid the bill, and they left the hotel and flagged a taxi. Leah had a beautiful apartment in the heart of the city, elegantly furnished and monitored by a doorman who, like Diane's, often wondered about what went on behind the heavy oak door leading to this mysterious woman's apartment. Leah and Wendy, their faces flushed with anticipation, swept past him and hurried for the elevator.

Leah couldn't wait once the apartment door was closed behind them. She took Wendy into her arms and pressed her mouth with a long, sultry kiss. Wendy opened her lips and pushed her tongue hard into Leah's mouth. The tall, elegant woman pressed her own just as hard, mingling with Wendy's tongue and moaning softly. She moved her hands up and down Wendy's back, grabbing at her firm ass before moving up to caress her again.

Wendy's own hands were on Leah, teasing her buttons open. Leah wore a lacy black bra and Wendy's fingers moved over it and played with the fabric. She dipped a finger behind it and gently rubbed against the hard nipple inside. Leah groaned and kissed Wendy hard, deeply, pressing her body up against her and trapping Wendy's hand between them with her fingers on that firm nub of flesh.

"Oh, hon, you feel so good," Leah whispered, and planted a row of tiny kisses on Wendy's neck before she returned to her sensuous mouth. "I want my tongue in your cunt. I want to taste your pussy."

"Come here, then," Wendy said, and led Leah over to an armchair. She sat her down, then knelt before her on the thick carpet and opened the rest of Leah's buttons. The black bra looked delicious against Leah's creamy skin.

Wendy sucked at her nipples through the fabric. They were so swollen and hard they stuck out firmly, and Wendy played with one while she tongued the other. She slipped her tongue in between Leah's breasts, and finally opened the tiny clasp in front and pushed the fabric away.

"Oh, you've got such beautiful tits," Wendy said, and sucked one into her mouth. At the same time, she slipped her hand under Leah's skirt and realized that she was wearing stockings. Slowly and teasingly, she ran her fingernails over Leah's thighs just above the stocking tops. Leah groaned and slouched into the chair, trying to position her pussy closer to Wendy's hand, but Wendy smiled and pulled back. "No use hurrying this," she said. "I've got all afternoon."

She sucked on Leah's nipples again, moving her hand closer and closer to the dark pussy that she wanted so badly. She teased unmercifully, rubbing one finger across the top of the hairline, then over Leah's thighs and back down to the tops of her stockings. She knew that once she did put her hand within that delicious triangle, she would find it hot and wet, waiting impatiently for her.

She decided to make Leah wait a little longer. She stood up and as Leah watched, she slowly unbuttoned her shirt, running her fingers over her exposed skin as her blouse opened a bit more each time. She was not wearing a bra, and she rubbed her nipples through the silk fabric before she finally pulled the shirt away from them. Her own nipples were as hard as Leah's and she pinched and played with them while Leah watched, nodding her approval and longing to hold them herself.

"They're going to feel so good when you get your hands on them," Wendy whispered, and she lifted them and held them out, just beyond Leah's reach.

"You bitch," Leah smiled. "You always did love to tease, didn't you? You wait until I'm between your legs. You'll be sorry."

Wendy's shirt was off now, and she unzipped her skirt and let it fall to the floor. Like Leah, she wore stockings with no panties, and her own dark bush looked hot and luscious. With a wicked smile on her face, she ran her hands through it, and pushed her fingers up between her pussy lips. "It's so hot and wet," she whispered. "It's just waiting for your tongue to be there."

"At times like this I wish you were a slave," Leah smiled. "Then I could just order you to bring that pussy over here."

"So you could," Wendy agreed, and she rubbed herself hard, enjoying the longing on Leah's face. "But just think about how good this is going to feel when you finally get close to it."

She played with herself for a bit longer. Her clit was throbbing and it felt wonderful to have her fingers on it, but she forced herself to pull her hand away. She was saving it for Leah. She knew how good Leah's tongue could feel on her, and she was looking forward to it as much as Leah was anticipating having Wendy's tongue on her.

She reached for Leah's hand, and the two of them went into the bedroom where Leah shed the rest of her clothes. Like Wendy, her body was firm and gorgeous, and when she stretched out on the bed, Wendy couldn't help but admire her for a moment before she bent down and ran her tongue from her nipples down to the dark hair between her legs.

She was just as much of a tease here. She used her tongue the same way she had used her fingers, to trace a circle around Leah's pussy over her belly and down to her thighs. The hot, rich aroma of Leah's cunt made her own throb wildly, but she resisted the temptation to bury her face in it. Instead she moved back and forth around it, until Leah was gasping and moaning with desire.

Finally she used her fingers to spread the swollen lips apart, and pushed her tongue against the hot clit. Leah shivered and moaned loudly as Wendy's tongue slowly ran up and down the length of her clit and then moved to the entrance of her hole.

"Oh, stick it in, hon," Leah whispered, and Wendy poked her tongue as far as she could into the wet hole. She then replaced her tongue with her finger, and Leah groaned as she pushed inside. The walls of Leah's vagina were hot and soft as velvet, but the muscles held her finger firmly as she pushed in and out. As she did, she flicked her tongue over Leah's clit, which was now so large it pushed out between her pussy lips. Gently Wendy sucked it in between her lips and nibbled on it with her teeth.

"Fuck my cunt!" Leah said, and Wendy pushed two fingers inside the velvet hole, then moved them back and forth rapidly. Her mouth never left Leah's huge clit and her own pussy was soaked. She ran her tongue up both sides of Leah's button, then flicked rapidly across it, pushing it back and forth as hard as she could. Leah's hips were moving, bringing her clit in contact with Wendy's tongue, and she groaned loudly as the hot rush went through her each time her clit was licked.

"Oh, that feels so good!" Leah groaned, as Wendy sucked hard on her clit. As she held it between her lips, she also teased the tip of it with her tongue. Leah was grinding her pussy against Wendy's mouth, pushing her hips toward the tongue that was doing such wonderful things to her cunt. Wendy's face was wet with pussy juice and the rich smell filled her nose. She tried to get as deep into Leah's cunt as she possibly could.

She could feel Leah trembling, and she stepped up her efforts. Her fingers were buried in Leah's smooth, wet hole, and her tongue was moving as fast as possible over Leah's hard clit. Leah stiffened and then cried out loudly as she came. Wendy stayed on her clit the whole time, as Leah's hips bucked and ground against her. Finally, when it was over, she gently lapped Leah's pussy and pulled her fingers out of her hole, sucking the thick, sweet juice off of them.

"Oh, girl, come up here," Leah said, and Wendy moved up on the bed and straddled her pussy over Leah's full, sensuous lips. The first touch of Leah's tongue on her throbbing pussy was a fire-and-ice sensation, so hot and sweet that if it had been any harder Wendy might have come right then.

Leah reached up to hold Wendy's ass, and she used her grip to move Wendy's pussy on her tongue. She licked up and down the sides of Wendy's clit, then tickled the entrance to her tunnel and finally moved back to flick her tongue against the tight hollow of Wendy's asshole.

"Oh, that's not fair!" Wendy said, as she realized that Leah intended to tease her by moving all around her most sensitive areas, skirting them to build up the pressure in Wendy's clit.

"Sure it is," Leah replied. "Remember who teased me?" She went back to her slow circling, and Wendy gasped as she was allowed a light touch on her clit.

The touch flicked away, though, and Wendy again enjoyed the sweet buildup as Leah's tongue snaked its way around her hole, pushing her pussy lips aside and running up and down the groove around her clit. Then, finally, as Wendy had done to her, Leah began to concentrate on Wendy's clit.

The hot, delicious rush up Wendy's spine was glorious as Leah's tongue worked over her pussy. Wendy groaned and pressed her hips down until her pussy was right on top of Leah's mouth. Leah lapped up her hot juice eagerly, then pushed her tongue against Wendy's clit again.

"Lick it right there!" Wendy gasped, and Leah responded by lapping quickly at Wendy's clit. One finger was massaging the opening to Wendy's hole. Wendy herself was playing with her tits, pinching and rolling the nipples between her fingers as the heat in her cunt spread throughout her whole body. This had definitely been worth waiting for.

The pressure in her belly and her pussy was almost unbearable, and she squeezed her nipples hard as she ground her cunt on Leah's tongue. The wave broke over her, and she moaned as her orgasm rushed all through her. When it was finally finished, she collapsed into Leah's arms, and the two of them kissed and caressed each other's satisfied bodies.

"You certainly had a good teacher," Wendy teased, as she cupped Leah's breast in her hand and rubbed it gently.

"I must have been a good student," Leah agreed, smiling. "I can even make a teacher come."

"Very well, too," Wendy purred. Her pussy was still sensitive and she shivered when Leah's hand brushed against it. She loved the warm feeling she had after an orgasm, when her whole body felt alive and tender.

Leah kissed her and stood up; Wendy admired her body as she stretched. Her beautiful tits stood straight out, her belly was firm and flat and her mound rose gently, covered with thick, delicious hair. Wendy felt her own hot pussy stirring again.

Going to the closet, Leah selected a heavy, white satin robe, which she draped over her shoulders. She offered Wendy a gorgeously patterned silk one, which Wendy put on, enjoying the slippery cool feeling as the fabric touched her skin. She sat back on the bed and watched Leah. The dark-haired woman didn't bother to tie her robe closed, and it hung open in front, giving Wendy tantalizing glimpses of sweet, hard nipples and dark, inviting bush.

Leah left the room, and Wendy heard her in the kitchen. A little while later, she returned with two china cups of coffee on a small tray. Wendy sipped hers as Leah opened a bedside drawer and took out a small book.

"I'm going to get those two over here," she said. "You can meet them and then we'll make arrangements for their classes."

"Excellent idea," Wendy said, putting her thin china cup down. It really was a good idea. She always preferred seeing how slaves interacted with their mistresses on their own ground, in familiar settings. It would give her an idea as to how she should focus their training, and give her some insight as to how the mistress would like her slave to behave. It would be especially helpful with Margot, the difficult one. Wendy thought that if she could meet this problematic woman with Leah there to give her orders, she might begin to understand why she was so un-slave-like when she claimed that being a slave was really what she wanted.

Leah looked up the first number and dialled. "Ellen, please," she said, and covered the receiver with her hand. "This one works in a small office," she told Wendy. "Naturally she can't call me 'Mistress' when I call her there. Each time I see her after speaking to her at work, I punish her for not using the proper form of address." Wendy smiled, and made a mental note to use such a trick in the future on her own slaves. She loved cruel little schemes such as that.

"Ellen? I believe you know who this is," Leah said. "Good. Ellen, I need you to come over here right away. This is very important and I will not be kept waiting."

She paused for a long time, and Wendy guessed that the woman on the other end was struggling for something to say. Her theory was verified when Leah said, "Repeat after me, Ellen. Oh, Mother, I'm so sorry, I forgot that I was supposed to drive you to your doctor's appointment today."

She paused again, and when she spoke, her voice had the ice-cold, steel-hard inflection of a mistress who expects to be obeyed implicitly. "You may show your appreciation when you arrive. Now hurry up. I know exactly how long it takes you to get from your office to here, and I will be timing you. There will be a lash for every half-minute you are late."

She hung up the phone and turned to Wendy. "That one is a breeze," she said. "She's so eager to please, she's almost the perfect slave already. The only thing wrong with her is her rough edges. She isn't fully versed in serving techniques and things like that. But I can't fault her sincerity."

"No problem," Wendy smiled. "When I'm finished with them, you will have two perfect slaves, both of them fine and polished. You'll be proud of both of them."

Leah took a sip of her coffee, then looked up another number in her book. "I hope you're right, Wendy," she said. "But I wouldn't be too sure until you get a good look at this one."

"Do they know about each other?" Wendy asked. "Have they met?"

"Oh, yes," Leah said, dialling the number. "I've always had at least two at all times. Margot's the newcomer, so it wasn't like she was being cast aside or anything. And Ellen doesn't seem to mind at all. She was a replacement for that blonde slave, the one who got transferred to another city. Then I got Margot, and Ellen became even more submissive and fawning. I guess she wanted to prove to me that she was better than the rookie. Unfortunately, so far she is."

There was an answer on the other end, and Leah's warm voice again took on its steely quality. "This is your Mistress, slave," she said. There was a slight pause.

"I need you here right away. I have someone you have to meet, and she won't be kept waiting. Neither will I." There was another pause, and Leah's face flushed a little. "I don't care, scum. I don't give a shit if you're scheduled for major surgery in three minutes. Either you show up here, right away, or you don't bother coming back ever again. Is that understood? Good. Now hurry up. If you're not here within half an hour, my door will be locked and will remain locked to you forever." She slammed down the phone.

"Trouble?" Wendy asked.

"Claims a dental appointment," Leah said. "See what I mean? I've found that the only way I can make her obey implicitly is to threaten to get rid of her."

"I expected that," Wendy said. An idea was forming in her mind, an insight into Margot's troubling character. "I think I'm beginning to understand just what's going on."

"I hope you're on the right track," Leah said. "I don't know why, but I'd hate to lose this one."

Wendy glanced at her watch. "How long before they arrive?"

"Ellen needs about twenty minutes to get here," Leah said. "If she hurries, Margot can be here just a few minutes after that. Why, do you have something in mind?"

"I certainly do," Wendy said, and reached over to the opening in Leah's satin robe. She took one of Leah's large breasts into her hand and massaged it, then sucked on the nipple. Leah groaned and stretched out beside Wendy. She untied Wendy's sash and her hand strayed down to that hot, wet spot between her legs.

Wendy pushed her own fingers between Leah's sex-swollen pussy lips. Both of their clits were still sensitive from their explosive orgasms, and even the lightest touches sent delicate chills from those hot nubs right up their spines.

"Finger me!" Leah whispered, and Wendy took the hard clit between her finger and thumb and gently rocked it back and forth. Leah's hand was massaging Wendy's clit as well and the two kissed deeply as they felt each other's pussies. Wendy's free hand found its way to Leah's nipple and she stroked and squeezed it gently as she slipped two fingers inside Leah's soaked tunnel.

"Oh, that feels good," Leah moaned as Wendy pushed her fingers deep into Leah's cunt. Her own pussy was on fire as Leah's hand moved quickly but delicately over her clit. She pushed her tongue into Leah's mouth as hard as she could. She wished she could have pushed it right down her throat. Leah met her and their tongues mingled, snaking over each other and sliding back and forth. The kiss muffled their moans and their hips were moving rapidly, putting their clits in direct contact with probing fingers.

Wendy's fingers were so wet with Leah's juices, they slipped effortlessly between her pussy lips, and she ran them up and down the grooves beside Leah's clit. When she pressed on the hard button, Leah moaned again and stepped up her efforts on Wendy's pussy.

They kept each other on the edge for a long time. There was a knock at the door and Leah pulled her hand away, but Wendy took it and firmly put it back between her legs. "It's only a slave, silly," she said, running her fingers over Leah's clit. "Make her wait."

Leah did. Wendy tickled the entrance to Leah's hole, then pushed two fingers inside. At the same time, her thumb rubbed hard over Leah's clit. Leah, meanwhile, was flicking her fingers on Wendy's clit, pushing it back and forth and pressing down on it with each stroke.

Wendy came first. The hot wave broke over her and she gasped and cried out, her hand still in Leah's cunt. She kneaded Leah's nipple while her other hand fucked Leah's cunt and rubbed her clit hard. It didn't take long before Leah was moaning too, thrashing her hips and trembling as she came.

They kissed gently a few more times, then got up off the bed, adjusted their robes, and walked into the living room.

Leah opened the door. Ellen was waiting in the hallway; at Leah's command she came inside, then automatically dropped to her knees in front of her mistress.

The blow came swiftly, and Ellen's cheek burned brightly where Leah's hand had slapped her. "I'm so sorry, Mistress!" she cried. "I wanted so badly to address you properly!"

"I really don't care," Leah replied coldly. "You may thank me for the excuse I gave you." Her feet were bare and Ellen bent down and kissed them reverently, slipping her tongue deftly between the toes.

"Get up," Leah ordered, and Ellen did. "Mistress Wendy is here. You have met her before."

"Yes, Mistress," Ellen said. She rushed over to Wendy and curtsied before her. "Good afternoon, Mistress Wendy."

Wendy nodded. She was pleased to see that Ellen was respectful to another mistress and that the curtsy seemed to come naturally to her. However, she also noted that Ellen had not dipped as low as she would have liked, and that she got up far too quickly. Wendy decided that a proper greeting would be one of Ellen's first lessons.

"Our coffee is cold," Leah said, and Ellen immediately rushed into the kitchen. Shortly afterward, she returned with freshly filled cups, and cream and sugar on a silver tray. The two women had seated themselves on the sofa, and Ellen placed the tray on the table before them. She mixed in cream and sugar to their specifications and then handed them the cups, kneeling before them, her eyes on the floor.

"You've given me some good material to work with," Wendy said, as she took the cup.

"I told you this one was pretty good," Leah agreed, speaking about Ellen as if she was still at her office and not kneeling before them. "Oh, I almost forgot. Ellen, take your clothes off."

"Yes, Mistress," Ellen replied, but in a very unhappy voice. She stole a quick glance at Wendy before she stood up to unbutton her blouse and skirt.

Her cheeks were bright red; Wendy wondered why, since Ellen hadn't seemed to mind being naked in front of her before. Indeed, it was the first time Wendy had ever seen her with clothes on.

Ellen stripped off her blouse. She was a very small woman, but her breasts were full and tipped with lovely rosy nipples. When she slipped the skirt off, Leah smiled and Wendy understood the embarrassment. "You may stop there, slave," Leah said.

Ellen whispered, "Thank you, Mistress," and again knelt on the floor. She was wearing a most ridiculous getup: a small pair of men's boxer shorts patterned with small red hearts.

"Other than washing them and bathing, you haven't taken them off, have you?" Leah demanded.

"No, Mistress," Ellen replied.

"You slept in them as well?"

"Yes, Mistress," came the whispered answer.

"For the whole week, as I commanded?"

"The whole week, Mistress," Ellen said.

Wendy smiled. "The hearts match your cheeks right now, slave," she said, enjoying the humiliation Ellen was feeling.

"Thank you, Mistress," Ellen replied, her eyes on the floor. Wendy could hardly wait to get this one under her command.

There was another knock on the door. "Get that," Leah commanded, and Ellen jumped up and ran to open the door. Leah noticed that she stood behind it, so that the visitor would not be able to see her. "Out in front!" Leah snapped, and Ellen stood in front of the door as she opened it, her whole face and neck red.

The woman at the door was stunning. Tall and slim, with shoulder-length brown hair, she wore a low-cut shirt that showed off the tops of her heavy, creamy breasts and a short skirt that put her long, well-shaped legs on display. She stepped inside, and as Ellen closed the door, the tall woman looked down at her with a condescending grin that spoke volumes. Ellen rushed back to her mistress and knelt before her; tears of shame and fury coursed down her scarlet cheeks, but she did not say a word.

"That's enough, Margot!" Leah snapped. "Now come in here."

Margot did, and in that instant Wendy was amazed. Her expression was sullen, as if she was sulking at having been ordered to do something. At the same time, her eyes were warm and filled with love as she looked at her mistress sitting on the sofa.

Her eyes changed right away when she noticed Wendy. As she took in the sight of the loosely fastened robes and the satisfied expressions on their faces, it became obvious that she knew what Wendy and Leah had just shared. Her swift glance at Wendy was cold and jealous.

"Margot, this is Mistress Wendy," Leah said.

Margot hardly glanced in Wendy's direction as she nodded her head. "Mistress," she said, then turned her attention back to Leah.

"I didn't tell you to come here so that I could look at your clothes," Leah said pointedly.

"Yes, Mistress," Margot said, and opened the few remaining buttons on her shirt. She was so maddeningly slow that it was obvious she was testing her mistress. Frustrated, Wendy had to suppress the urge to leap up and strike her to the ground for her impudence. If she were mine, Wendy thought, she'd be black and blue right now. Then she realized that soon this woman *would* be hers to train and control, and the thought made her smile. It amazed her how much she was looking forward to making this woman knuckle under. She would lay that smooth back right open if necessary, but she was determined that she was going to win this one.

Slowly the bra came off. Margot's breasts were large, but very firm with hard nipples. She had a model's perfectly sculpted body, right down to her beautiful dark triangle which took forever to be uncovered. Wendy had to admit that she was one of the most admirable looking slaves she had ever seen. The thought of that body wearing a collar and shackles turned her on, and a picture of Margot strapped to the X-frame and feeling the cruel ends of a cat-o'-nine-tails had her hot all over again.

"On your knees," Leah ordered. Again, the order was carried out with an infuriating slowness. Wendy noticed that the slow actions were totally at odds with the look of love and devotion on the woman's face. She decided to test her theory.

"Don't you think," she said to Leah, "that those two commands were carried out a bit too slowly?"

"I think you're right," Leah said. She caught onto Wendy's plan right away. "Yes, you are right. I think we'll have to do something about that."

Wendy noticed that Margot's eyes lit up like candles. She drew her breath in and her eyes followed her mistress' every move as Leah got up and walked over to an antique writing desk across the room. Tucked into a drawer was a piece of rubber hose. Wendy saw Margot's eyes close in passion and a smile cross her lips.

"On your hands and knees!" Leah ordered. Wendy noticed that there was none of the insolent slowness this time; Margot was on all fours swiftly and it seemed that she arched her back to present her ass fully to her mistress.

The rubber hose landed with a loud thud, and

Margot gasped. Wendy could well imagine how much the blow must have hurt. Still kneeling on the floor, Ellen looked over fearfully, terrified that the hose might also land on her. But Margot's eyes were tightly closed and even though the hose had formed a large welt on her ass, her lips still held the hint of a smile.

Thwack! The hose found its target again. Margot was trembling and her eyes were screwed shut, but only a tiny moan escaped her. This time the hose hit her back, and her skin welled up a painful red. There was a bit of moisture in her eyes, but it was obvious she was enjoying herself.

Wendy was surprised at the punishment Margot could take. Her ass and back were crossed with welts so big and red that Wendy felt her excitement rising as she looked at them. Yet only a quiet groan escaped her when the hose struck.

Leah lifted her arm again and brought the hose down as hard as she could. This one must have really hurt, for two small tears moved down Margot's cheeks. Her face was as red as the welts, but still she held her ass out for Leah to punish. Leah brought the hose down three more times and finally a sob escaped the tall woman. Her back and her ass were so red they looked burned and blistered.

"Kneel," Leah ordered, and again Margot obeyed her swiftly. Leah put the hose back in its drawer, then stepped in front of Margot. The punished slave looked up at her devotedly.

"Leah, would you go into the kitchen for a moment?" Wendy asked. Leah did, and Wendy watched as Margot followed her every move until she was out of sight. Once she was gone, Margot's expression changed again, and Wendy thought she looked just like an abandoned puppy. When Leah came back out, Margot's face once again became radiant as she caught a glimpse of her mistress.

"You two into the bedroom," Leah ordered as she sat down. Ellen sprang up instantly, read to obey; back to her old habits, Margot got up slowly and shuffled toward the bedroom. It was obvious that she resented being forced to leave while Wendy was left behind with her mistress.

"So what's your opinion?" Leah asked.

"Well, I'm no psychologist, but I think I've found the answer," Wendy said. "You've never looked at her face while you're beating her, have you?"

"No," Leah replied.

"She's in ecstasy. She absolutely loves everything you give her. I think if she had a wish, she'd ask for a bigger hose," Wendy said. "I haven't seen a slave that fond of pain in a long time. Part of the problem is that she's just begging to be punished."

"So what's the rest of it?"

"She absolutely adores you," Wendy continued. "She was like a little lost soul when you went into the kitchen. I really think she does a lot of it to get your attention. When you're punishing her, it's obvious that you're paying attention to her. So she demands punishment by misbehaving."

"Well, that's fine that she likes punishment, but she's getting on my nerves," Leah said. "I like doling out punishment, too—when it's called for. But I don't think I have to wear my arm out every time I want a cup of coffee brought to me. She needs to be taught that I'm not going to put up with it."

"Well, she's still testing you," Wendy said. "You mentioned that threatening to get rid of her makes her obey instantly. Right now it's the one thing she's really afraid of. Whenever she misbehaves, you beat her right away, don't you?"

"Instantly," Leah said.

"Maybe we can try ignoring her completely when she does something wrong. It's the attention she craves. And I'm going to try to find a punishment that's beyond what she enjoys. Maybe then she will fear punishment as well as anticipate it. When you can get them looking forward to it and dreading it at the same time, you've got them around your little finger. She's not at that point yet. In that respect, she's as green as a slave that's only put on a collar for the first time."

Leah smiled. "It sounds so obvious, I'm surprised I never noticed it," she said. "I guess you need someone else to look at it from a different perspective. So, do you think she's worth it?"

"Oh, definitely," Wendy replied. "Actually, Leah, she's magnificent. I'm a little jealous that you found her before I did. I really think that once her spirit is tamed, she will be superb."

Leah called the two to come back, and they did, kneeling before the dominatrixs sitting on the sofa.

"Mistress Wendy is the teacher I was telling you about," Leah said. "You will be attending her classes regularly. There will be no excuse for absenteeism. The first time I hear that you are not in class, you will also not be stepping through my door again. Understood?"

"Yes, Mistress!" Ellen replied quickly. By her expression it was obvious that it never occurred to her to play hooky from Wendy's school. Her mistress had ordered her to attend, and attend she would.

Margot was a different story. It was just as obvious that she did not want to have anything to do with Wendy and her classes. But the threat of being dismissed entirely was too much for her. "Yes, Mistress," she replied.

"When you are with Mistress Wendy, it is the same as being with me," Leah continued. "You will obey her no matter what the command. She will punish you however she sees fit, and I don't care how severely she does so. How she treats you is none of my concern. The only thing I care about is that you do the very best you can. I will not be ashamed of my slaves at any time while they are students in Mistress Wendy's school."

Wendy stood up and walked behind the two who knelt before her on the floor. "Your mistress has instructed me that both of you will graduate as perfect slaves," she said. "That's obvious because only perfect slaves will ever leave my school. The question is how long it will take, and that is entirely up to you."

She walked behind Ellen and flicked a finger on her cheek. "I like your respect, slave," she said. "You have a lot of it. Unfortunately, you don't know how to use it. Your greeting to me was too quick. You carried the coffee sloppily. You will need a fair bit of fine-tuning."

She walked behind Margot. "You are another kettle of fish altogether," she said. "You think that this whole idea of going to school is a joke, don't you? My dear, I am going to prove you wrong."

She reached down and touched Margot's cheek just as she had touched Ellen's. Unlike the smaller slave, Margot shrank back to avoid Wendy's fingers.

Wendy was upon her instantly. She grabbed a huge handful of hair and yanked it back hard until Margot's head was forced backward, her eyes level with Wendy's. She gasped loudly; she hadn't imagined that Wendy could move so quickly that she could get the better of her. Wendy realized this and was thrilled by the knowledge.

When she spoke, her voice was so filled with restrained fury that even Leah was shocked.

"There are three things that can happen, worm," she hissed. "One is that the slave will get the better of the teacher, and the teacher will have to give in. That will never happen, and the faster you get that through your skull the better.

"Second is that the slave and the teacher are equal and that no one wins. You can get that one out of your head, too.

"Third is that the slave learns just who her superior is. Your superior happens to be any mistress who gives you a command, whether it's your Mistress Leah, or it's me, or it's any other mistress who stoops low enough to speak with you. You might like the sounds of the first two options, but let me give you a little reality, scum. The only thing that's going to happen is that you are going to learn some respect, and you are going to learn it in my classroom whether you like it or not. Your feelings don't mean anything to me. The only thing that matters is that you are going to learn your place." Using the handful of hair, Wendy threw Margot to the ground. Shocked by Wendy's speed and strength, Margot stayed there, looking at Wendy with a new expression: one of wonder and just a little excitement.

"Tomorrow evening, six o'clock," Wendy told them both. "Your mistress will give you the directions. She has warned you what will happen if you do not show up. Let me also warn you that there are dire consequences for being late." She sat down beside Leah on the sofa. Margot was still sprawled on the floor. "Get up, slave," she ordered. Although she did it slowly, Margot did rise up to a kneeling position, and both of them knew that the first battle had been won.

"Now both of you get out of here," Leah ordered. "Mistress Wendy and I have things to do." Ellen gratefully pulled her clothes up over the heart-patterned boxer shorts. Margot put her clothes on as well, sullen now that her session with her beloved mistress was over, a session that she had to share with both the small slave and the teacher who would be training her. If her clothes rubbed painfully on her bruised flesh, she showed no sign of it.

When the door closed behind the slaves, Wendy turned to Leah. "You know, you really are pretty good with that rubber hose," she said.

"You really think so?" Leah asked. Her hand was again straying over to the opening of the silk robe.

"I really do," Wendy said, and she stood up, offering her hand to Leah. "Come on in. We'll discuss it." She led Leah back to the bedroom, her pussy throbbing. She could hardly wait for her first full class to begin.

SIX

Wendy bunched up one of her black stockings, slipped her toes into it, and slowly pulled it up one long leg. When it was completely unrolled on her long leg, she bent and fastened it into her garter, then put on the other one and carefully attached it as well to the black leather garter strap.

Her whole outfit was supple, buttery-smooth leather. Her bra held her large breasts in place, and the nipples peeked through holes at the end. Black leather panties were visible under the leather garter belt, and a studded leather belt encircled her waist. She pulled on her favorite stiletto-heeled boots, then picked up her riding crop and walked down the hallway to the closed classroom door. She walked slowly, confidently. She knew the tapping of her heels on the hardwood floor would be heard through the closed door. She also knew that five women would be listening, waiting, anticipating, and dreading her entry all at the same time.

She opened the door. All five were kneeling on the hard floor in a row, as she had ordered. She smiled and closed the door behind her. "Good evening, class," she said, and walked to the front of the room.

"Good evening, Mistress," the voices chimed. Wendy looked at them approvingly as they knelt, their eyes on the floor.

All were naked, and wearing the leather collars that signified they were students. Brenda, Alicia and Leslie were completely submissive, kneeling motionless, their backs straight, their eyes down. Ellen shifted slightly, not used to the hard floor but trying desperately to please her teacher. She had been given permission by Leah to forsake the red-hearted boxer shorts and her sweet little body pleased Wendy very much.

She looked over at Margot. As she expected, the tall, stunning slave was glancing sideways, looking over her environment, adjusting her position on the floor, her expression sullen. As Wendy had imagined, the collar around her neck looked wonderful. It set off her perfect body, the unyielding leather circle harsh against the supple, smooth skin. Wendy wanted to grab it in her fist and drag her around by it. She smiled; she knew that soon enough, Margot would give her reason to do it.

"I'm glad to see everyone here and in their positions," Wendy said. She stepped over and gave Ellen a quick flick with the riding crop. It was just a reminder, a tap with the end, which stung and left a small reddish glow on the skin. "Don't squirm, Ellen," she said. "Slaves must sit perfectly still until they are told by their mistresses that they may move.

You look like a child that needs to go to the bathroom, not like a trained slave. I will not tolerate that."

"I'm sorry, Mistress," Ellen whispered, and kept as still as she could.

"As most of you are aware," Wendy continued, "none but perfect slaves will graduate from this school—or as perfect as you worthless things can become. And only graduates will have a special honor bestowed upon them to prove that they have graduated. Your mistresses will be thrilled when they see you with this honor. I don't believe I have to tell you what might happen if you fail my school and disgrace them."

She walked over to where a small wooden console was set up with a television set and a video player. "Some of you may be wondering just what I mean by a perfect slave. Since none of you are even close to that goal, I have some examples to show you. This is what you should be aiming for. This is the only type of behavior that will allow you to graduate and earn your honor."

She switched the television set on. The tape was one that had been given to her by Julie, the owner of the leather boutique. Wendy had already watched it once and had been so excited she had put her hand between her legs and rubbed her hot, wet pussy until she came.

The first portion of the tape had been shot at a dominatrixs' convention held in a large downtown hotel. Wendy was at first fascinated by all the different costumes worn by the mistresses. There were women in leather corsets, in tight leather dresses, in business suits, in wild outfits made of straps and chains, in romantic lacy dresses, in tight jeans and T-shirts.

The five slaves on the floor also watched the screen, captivated by what they saw. Each mistress had at least one slave, and many had two, three, or even four attending her. Like the mistresses, the slaves were in all types of uniforms and costumes, including a pair of delicious blonde twins who wore only leather cuffs on their wrists and sparkling jeweled collars around their throats, finished with gold chains held in their mistress' hand.

"Look at them carefully," Wendy said. "Watch how they behave."

The behavior of all of the slaves was beyond reproach. The camera focused on one slave wearing a leather mask, with holes for her eyes, nose, and mouth. The woman was fetching a glass of champagne for her leather-clad mistress; she carried it perfectly and bowed slightly, eyes down, as she offered it. Her mistress took it from her, and the slave bowed again, then immediately took her place behind her mistress.

"I have attended functions such as this in the past," Wendy told her captive audience. "I did not take any slave whose behavior I questioned even slightly. In a room filled with other mistresses with perfectly trained slaves, I would only take the very best slave I had.

"It is an honor for a slave to be allowed to attend such an event," she continued. "You will not even be considered unless you are as good as the slaves you see here. If I were you, I would make it my goal to become as well trained as the slaves in this film."

The camera moved through the crowd in the hotel. There was a slave, dressed in a coarse peasant's dress, who knelt at her mistress' heel while her mistress, beautifully dressed in an expensive suit, spoke with another mistress. Suddenly, the mistress turned around and gave a command. The slave leaped up and quickly walked away, returning moments later with a drink for her mistress. Once the drink was accepted, the slave once again knelt at her mistress' feet.

"You will notice that each mistress has her preference when it comes to specific behavior," Wendy said. "One mistress might like her slave to kneel at all times, another might like something else. That doesn't matter; what does matter is that no matter what the command, it is carried out swiftly and without question."

She turned the television off. "We'll save the rest for a little later," she said. "First we will have a lesson."

She indicated a small table against the far wall, where a champagne glass filled with water had been set. "I want each of you to go and get that glass and bring it back to me. Imagine that we are at the function you just watched. Imagine that the whole room is filled with other mistresses and other slaves."

She motioned for Ellen to go first. The small woman hurried over and picked up the glass by the bottom of the stem, then brought it to the leather-clad teacher, who was still carrying her riding crop. Wendy noticed that she quickly glanced at the crop as she bowed before her teacher, offering the glass.

To Ellen's relief, the crop stayed down. "Good," Wendy said. "Next time, though, place your free hand on your thigh when you bow. It makes a much neater presentation."

"Yes, Mistress," Ellen said. Wendy motioned for her to return the glass to the table. "Thank you, Mistress."

Leslie, Alicia, and Brenda all brought the glass over; Brenda earned an extra bit of praise for her quick bow before she went to get the glass. Her first lesson had not been forgotten, and she did not allow even a flicker of pride to cross her face.

"Your turn, Margot," Wendy said, bracing herself for the first confrontation. "Bring the glass over here."

Margot was in fine form. She glanced at the other slaves, kneeling on the floor in a straight line, then slowly got up. She stood before Wendy, but did not give the small bow that had earned Brenda praise. She then walked across the room, slowly, and picked up the glass.

Brenda, Alicia, and Leslie looked shocked at this new pupil's behavior. Ellen, who knew what to expect, simply looked disgusted. Margot carried the glass by the stem, but when she presented it to Wendy, there was no bow, no display of submission; she simply offered the glass the same way Wendy might have given a drink to another mistress.

"That will do, Margot," Wendy said coldly. "Now put it back."

As Margot turned to go, the riding crop struck her across the backs of her thighs. Wendy was thrilled to see her jump, and the hard blow left a thin red welt across both legs.

Margot stopped instantly and stood, waiting. But Wendy simply tucked the crop under her arm. "Put it back, slave," she said. "We don't have all night." Margot stood for a second longer, then walked back across the room and replaced the glass on the table. When she came back and took her place in line, Wendy could see disappointment on her face. Wendy congratulated herself for holding back and denying Margot the additional punishment she had expected. Margot glanced up and caught Wendy's eye for a moment. In that split second, she realized why she had only received the one blow, and she put her eyes back down.

First round goes to me, you worthless bitch, Wendy thought to herself as she turned to the blackboard and began writing the names of different types of wines. She drilled the five for a few minutes on their knowledge, gave them a quick oral test, and then ordered Brenda to go into the kitchen and bring her a glass of wine. Brenda's eyes were almost moist as she thanked her mistress for the honor and rushed out of the room. While she waited for her drink to arrive, Wendy arranged several different restraints at the front of the room. She could see Margot's eyes light up.

On a small table at the front, she had placed lengths of rope, handcuffs, leather cuffs with snap rings, some very evil-looking thumbscrews joined together, and a canvas straitjacket.

"The type of restraint your mistress will use determines the position you will take when you stand before her," Wendy said. "Brenda, come up here."

The blonde-haired slave quickly stood up and hurried to stand before her beloved mistress. Wendy smiled. The competition in the room was helping to ensure that Brenda would learn her lessons fully and retain them completely. Wendy was sure that she would be very pleased with her own property once all had graduated.

Wendy picked up a length of rope. "For ropes, it is easiest if the wrists are crossed," she said. She nodded, and Brenda held out her arms in the proper fashion, a method she had learned from Wendy even before the school had been set up. Swiftly, deftly, Wendy lashed her slave's wrists together. "You see how pleasing it is to the mistress if everything is ready for her," Wendy said. "Now let me see all of you take this position." Four sets of wrists went out, properly crossed; even Margot was swift to do it properly. "Good, good," Wendy said, and she untied Brenda's wrist and sent her back to kneel on the floor.

Alicia got the handcuffs, and the pupils were taught several ways to present their wrists both in front and behind themselves, and several hand positions. Once again, Wendy noticed that Margot was extremely attentive, and swift to hold her hands in each of the new positions.

Leslie was the model for the leather cuffs, while Ellen got the thumbscrews. Wendy was not easy with them, and by the end of the demonstration, tears were visible on Ellen's cheeks. The thumbscrews themselves held Ellen's hands together by attaching to each thumb with nasty screws that pressed painfully into her flesh. By the look on Margot's face, it was obvious that she was very disappointed that the screws were not biting into her own thumbs.

Finally it was Margot's turn, and the sullen slow movements were gone; she was on her feet and standing before Wendy in a flash to receive the straitjacket. Wendy surprised her by being very gentle as she positioned Margot's arms to show the rest of the class how to stand in preparation for receiving the jacket. When she slipped the jacket on, she did so carefully, and she was careful to position Margot's arms rather than yank them into place, as she so dearly longed to do. Once the jacket was in place, Wendy made a few comments to the rest of the class, then unstrapped it and removed it from the gorgeous slave as gently as she could. Once Margot was naked again, save for the chrome-ringed leather collar, Wendy indicated that she could join her place in the lineup.

Such a change! Wendy noted with satisfaction that Margot's cheeks were bright red, whether from shame or frustration Wendy didn't know. Her eyes looked dull and hurt, almost like she was going to cry. Her expression was one of confusion. The teacher she had expected to be so cruel had actually been nice to her! Wendy smiled. Round two, she thought to herself. Soon you will be groveling before my feet and you won't even know what hit you.

She took a sip of the wine Brenda had brought for her, and tried to come up with a plan for round three. It came to her as she was putting the restraints back in their spots on the wall.

"Now, slaves," she said, as she walked back up to the blackboard in front of them, "something that you should definitely know is how to treat your mistress when she comes home. There is a pattern you should follow, and I expect that by next class you will have it memorized."

She wrote each item down on the blackboard. "First you must greet your mistress properly, holding the door for her, taking her coat and her bag, making sure that her chair is ready," Wendy said. "When she sits down, you ask permission to remove her shoes. When that permission is granted, you do so. If they are dirty, you ask permission to clean them. If you are told to do so with your tongue, then you do it—and thank your mistress for the privilege of doing so." She could see Margot catch her breath at the thought of being forced to lick the city grime off of the soles of Leah's shoes.

"You put those shoes away carefully, and you ask your mistress for permission to bring her some refreshment. If she grants you permission, you bring her whatever she wants, carried properly and served with a bow. Then you ask permission to do anything else your mistress might want you to do to make her more comfortable. She might ask for a pillow, or for assistance in putting on her robe, or for you to run a hot bath for her, or even for you to put your tongue in her pussy. No matter what the request is, you fulfill it immediately, you thank her for the privilege of doing it, and you do it correctly. There is simply no other way."

She pulled a chair over and stood beside it. "We will have a demonstration," she said. "I am just coming home, and I wish to be greeted properly by my slave. Let's see—Margot, you will show us how it's done."

Margot looked very slowly at the other four slaves, then got to her feet. It was just what Wendy and Ellen had expected, but Brenda, Alicia and Leslie stared, open-mouthed, at her insolent manners. They could not believe that any slave would not snap to attention once a command had been given.

Wendy had not only expected it, but had hoped that Margot would pull her famous act. She smiled, but it was an icy, bitterly cruel smile. Brenda saw it and felt her skin grow cold. She knew full well the fury that her mistress was holding in, and also knew that there was a plan under way. There was no other explanation for her mistress' leniency, and Brenda shivered, thankful that she was not on the receiving end of Wendy's wrath. It would be swift and very brutal.

The stunningly gorgeous slave stood before Wendy, her weight on one foot, her spine bent, looking more like an arrogant teenager than a submissive slave. Wendy took it in, but said nothing. She sat in the chair.

"I will already assume that you have taken my coat and greeted me," Wendy said. "You may now ask permission to remove my shoes."

Margot paused for a second before she said, "Mistress, may I remove your shoes?"

"You may," Wendy said.

Margot slowly bent in front of Wendy and touched her hand to the top of the beautiful stiletto-heeled boots. Without warning, Wendy gave a massive kick, and Margot was knocked onto her back. Before she could even register what had happened, Wendy was upon her, one strong fist grabbing the stout leather collar.

Margot didn't even attempt to rise, and Wendy dragged her along the wooden floor by the collar. The other four slaves watched.

"You still think that you can get the better of me, don't you, scum?" Wendy hissed. "I thought we went over your options before. There is only one thing that is going to happen here, and that is that you are going to leave this school perfectly trained and nothing less. Well, dogshit, your training begins now."

Margot was a tall woman, but Wendy was much more powerful, and she hauled the recalcitrant slave across the room to the padded horse. Pulling her by the collar, Wendy lifted her up and threw her across the horse. "Move and you're dead," she said, and got leather cuffs for her wrists and ankles.

The cuffs were on in seconds, and Wendy had to stop for a moment and admire them. The black leather and chrome rings looked so good against the firm flesh. Then she snapped them in place on the horse, so that Margot was bent over, her ass in the air, her head facing the floor.

Wendy then walked back to the front of the class. "This demonstration is actually going much better than I had planned," she told the four remaining slaves, all of whom looked terrified of her, wondering if her rage would be vented on them as well. "Not only will we learn how to greet our mistress, but we will also learn what might happen if we don't do a good job."

She then went back to the lesson, this time selecting Leslie to demonstrate how to properly greet her mistress. To her delight, the novice slave performed adequately and only required a tap with the riding crop when her bow was not as deep as Wendy would have liked. From across the room, she could hear Margot's heavy, excited breathing, and the occasional click of the chrome snaps against the steel rings. She could imagine Margot's frustration at being lashed to the horse with no further punishment. She continued the lesson, determined that she was going to win all three rounds during the evening's class. Margot's face was already red and every so often she would pull back against her bonds, as if testing them. At one point, Alicia stole a glance back at her, and received a blow across her cheek that snapped her head sideways. Wendy was determined that everyone in the room would ignore Margot until she was almost beside herself with the desire to be whipped.

The captive slave was left alone for a half hour, while Wendy continued the regular lessons. By this time she could see that Margot's pussy was glistening and her nipples were as hard as rocks.

Wendy walked to her wall of devices and carefully selected a large nine-tailed leather whip. After discussing the problem with Leah, she had come to the conclusion that while Margot enjoyed being punished, she hadn't really received anything brutal. The cat, she thought, would go a long way in breaking this slave's spirit.

"Now, all of you are going to watch this," she

told the other four, and they obediently turned around. "I want you to know that naughty pupils don't just sit in the corner when they're bad in my class. I want you to see what will really happen."

She then lifted the whip and with all the strength in her arm, brought it down on Margot's back. It landed with a gut-wrenching slap of leather on skin. She was right; Margot had never experienced anything like this before. A loud cry escaped her lips, then a moan.

Wendy felt her own pussy throb as she looked at her handiwork. Nine perfect welts rose on the skin as the blood welled up under it. With the second cruel blow, several thin lines of blood appeared on Margot's back.

Whap! Again the bitter lash came down. The other four slaves winced when it fell, and Ellen looked so white that Wendy thought she might faint.

Indeed, the punishment had been more than even Margot had expected. Her face was streaming with tears and she was sobbing loudly. "Mistress!" she cried. "Please, Mistress, mercy!" The words were as sweet as honey to Wendy's ears, and she smiled as she brought the whip down again.

Margot could hardly speak now for her sobs, and Wendy heard only part of her request for leniency. Once more her arm went up, and the cat-o'-nine-tails came down a final time, drawing several more thin lines of blood. Then Wendy threw the whip aside and went back to the front of the classroom.

She spoke calmly over Margot's sobs and gasps for breath. "I believe you all get the point," she said. "There are very clear-cut lines in a mistress-slave relationship, and those lines become even clearer when the mistress decides that it's time for punishment. Any questions? No? Very good. Now Alicia, tell me, when your mistress asks for red wine, what type of glass do you use?"

Seemingly oblivious to Margot's discomfort, Wendy went on with the lesson. When it was over, she walked back to the horse and unsnapped the wrist cuffs that held the beaten slave to it. She hauled Margot up by her collar, over the horse and down on the floor. Still attached to the horse by her ankle cuffs, Margot sat up, facing it. Her face was covered with tears and mucus, and her back was striped with welts and thin lines of blood.

Wendy looked at her with disgust. "You make me sick," she said. She got a scrap of rag from a hook on the wall. "Clean yourself up. You look like a baby with a runny nose." Margot wiped her face off. Her eyes were red-rimmed from crying and her cheeks were swollen.

Wendy wasn't sure if the battle was completely over, but she knew she had made some major inroads with that lesson. She snatched the rag away from the slave; it was wet in the middle. She tied it over Margot's eyes where it made an effective, if somewhat disgusting blindfold.

She returned to the television set at the front of the classroom. "I promised you more of this," she said. "This part will be a little treat for you. Those of you who performed adequately this evening will be allowed to watch it. Those who didn't will have to miss it." Margot, facing the horse, her eyes blindfolded, hung her head. Wendy's words had not been wasted on her.

Wendy turned the tape on. They watched the last few moments of the dominatrix convention; then the tape switched to an elegantly furnished room. A young, slim, blonde woman was kneeling on the thick carpet. She wore a leather collar around her throat, and there were cruel steel clamps on each nipple. There were straps around her waist that reached down between her legs. As the camera moved around, the slaves instantly noted that it was a chastity belt. Wendy smiled as she watched the obedient line of pupils, all kneeling on the hardwood floor. Their eyes were glued to the screens, their attention riveted to the screen. In the corner Margot was quietly sobbing.

The camera moved all around the kneeling slave. The slaves noticed that a heavy steel chain was attached to her collar and it hung down along her spine. The black chastity belt was tight against her buttocks and they noticed that she had thin leather cuffs around her ankles. Wendy smiled; she loved the sight of a well-outfitted slave kneeling so motionless, so submissively. One day her whole class, Margot included, would be just as good.

The camera focused again, from the front, on the cruel clamps, on the tight collar. Then it pulled back for a wider shot, and a tall black mistress walked in and stood beside her slave.

The four slaves watching the camera all drew in their breath. The mistress was gorgeous with an icy expression and a confident manner. She wore the same cruel, razor-sharp stilettos that Wendy favored, and her suit was made entirely of straps and rings. Each nipple pressed out from inside a chrome ring, and the straps that held them in place crisscrossed her body and made her breasts stand out perfectly. Her delicious dark triangle was complemented by the dark straps and the bright rings: Each slave longed to be able to obey her commands and place their tongues there. Long leather gauntlets ran up each arm, leaving her fingers exposed, showing off her long, perfectly lacquered, blood red nails.

"My boots are dirty, slave," she said. Her voice was as cold and sharp as a shard of broken glass.

"Yes, Mistress," the slave replied, and instantly she was on the floor. The slaves winced, imagining the sharp stab of pain once those nipple clamps were pressed into the carpet by her weight. But the blonde woman didn't even seem to notice; she was too intent on the shiny, patent-leather boots.

Her tongue snaked out and licked all over one of her mistress' feet. The black woman lifted it up, and the blonde woman's eyes were closed in ecstasy as she lapped the grime off the sole. She sucked the thin heel into her mouth, trying to take in as much of it as she possibly could. Then she moved up the boot, as her mistress put her foot back on the floor. The boots reached up to her mistress' thigh and she sat up to clean the tops of them.

The excitement was obviously too much for her, and her tongue strayed off the leather and onto the rich, smooth skin of the black woman's leg. Instantly, the mistress' expression changed from one of satisfaction to one of displeasure. Again, Wendy heard the slaves gasp, knowing that there was something very wrong.

Indeed there was. Swiftly the mistress reached down and grabbed one of the cruel clamps that bit into her slave's nipple. The red-nailed hand turned and twisted the clamp hard. The blonde slave cried out in agony.

"That isn't my boot, slave!" the woman hissed. "You were told to lick my boots. Now do as you're told!"

"Yes, Mistress!" the slave sobbed. The mistress let go of the clamp, and the slave slumped for a moment, swallowing hard as the pain returned to a dull throb. Then once again her tongue was on the patent leather, licking every inch of the tall boots.

"You will notice," Wendy interjected, "how quickly the mistress was able to grab the nipple clamp and twist it." Her words were not meant for the four kneeling before her; for them it had been obvious. The object of her lesson was still strapped to the horse, blindfolded and unable to watch the scene that would have been such a treat. Wendy smiled when she saw Margot slump a little and draw in her breath. Knowing that she was missing such an exciting scene must have been almost as painful as the whipping; Wendy felt like she was rubbing salt into those bloody welts.

Slowly and carefully, the slave licked clean the second boot, lapping the sole when it was lifted and sucking on the sharp heel before moving up to wash the rest of it. This time her tongue stayed on the leather and did not venture onto her mistress' skin. The slaves could see that the twisted nipple was still bright red from its ordeal, although both breasts must have still been throbbing and aching from the steel clamps that had not yet been removed.

"Now stand up," the mistress ordered when her boots were completely cleaned and polished by her charge's hot tongue.

The slave did so. The mistress grabbed both nipple clamps and pulled on them. Wendy noticed that Leslie closed her eyes as the woman's breasts were stretched out by the horrible clamps. Immediately Wendy walked behind her and slapped her hard on the side of her head. "Open your eyes," she ordered. "This was given to you as a treat and you are going to enjoy it."

"I'm sorry, Mistress," Leslie cried, and watched the screen. As she watched the tall black woman torture her blonde slave, she had to admit to herself that it was more and more exciting all the time. The cruelty that she had closed her eyes to was slowly starting to make her pussy throb.

The mistress pulled on the clamps until tears ran from her slave's eyes. Then she snapped them off. The blonde woman shrieked and put her hands to her bruised nipples. Oblivious to her pain, the mistress reached behind and grabbed the steel chain that was snapped to the collar.

"How convenient," the mistress crooned. "You already have your collar and leash on. Now down on all fours like the dog that you are." Sobbing, the slave obeyed.

The camera following her movement, the mistress started to walk around the room. Her steps were long, and the blonde woman had to hurry to keep up with her, moving along on her hands and knees. At one point, she fell behind and was rewarded with a hard pull on the chain.

The camera moved behind them, and Wendy could clearly see how ingenious the chastity belt was. It was open to allow the slave her toilet functions, but there was no way that she could play with herself once the device was in place. It looked extremely interesting, and Wendy made a mental note to ask Julie to order a couple for her. They might come in handy some time.

There was much more on the tape, but Wendy walked up and snapped the television set off. The slaves were clearly disappointed, but they did not dare complain.

"I think that's enough for tonight," Wendy said. The four remained in place, watching the blank screen, while she went back to the horse. She pulled off the rag that had served as a blindfold, then unsnapped Margot's ankles from the horse.

"Stand up," Wendy ordered, and Margot did so

meekly. "Take your place." The tall woman walked back and knelt in the lineup—much slower than Wendy would have liked, but faster than she had done before. Wendy knew that there was still a lot of spirit in this slave, but this lesson had gone a long way toward vanquishing it.

"I will give you permission to leave now," Wendy said, "all except for Brenda. You stay behind."

"Thank you, Mistress," the other four said. Wendy noticed that Margot was a bit slower than the others, but she had still chimed in.

The four slaves rose and walked out the door. Wendy waited until they had dressed, then she saw them out of the house. "Good night, Mistress," all four of them said, even Margot. Wendy noticed that she walked carefully, in great pain, and before she put on her coat, Wendy saw a few drops of blood seep through her white shirt. Once again, Wendy could feel her excitement rising.

She closed the door, then went back to the classroom. Brenda was still kneeling obediently on the hard floor. "Come with me, slave," Wendy said, and the blonde submissive got up and followed her mistress into the living room.

Once there, Wendy pulled off the soft leather panties, and Brenda could hardly believe her good fortune as she watched her mistress stretch out on the sofa, her legs apart and her beautiful dark pussy exposed. "Your tongue, slave," Wendy ordered.

Brenda needed no further orders. Within seconds she was on her knees on the carpet in front of the couch, her head between Wendy's legs. Wendy shivered slightly at the first touch of Brenda's hot tongue on her throbbing clit.

As always, Brenda knew the right spots. Her probing tongue found its way between the sweet secrets of Wendy's pussy lips, and back to her hole. She pressed her tongue inside the velvet tunnel and moved it back and forth, fucking her mistress deeply with her mouth. Wendy put her head back on the pillow and closed her eyes. It was so enjoyable being able to control her pleasure and order her pussy eaten any time she felt like it!

For her part, too, Brenda was thrilled. It was obvious to her that she was still her mistress' personal slave and not just another student in the classroom. She lapped heartily at her mistress' pussy, her tongue coated with her mistress' thick, creamy, delicious juice. Inside the classroom, she had to act just as the other slaves did, those slaves whose mistresses had paid for the privilege of having their slaves at Wendy's feet; but outside, it was she who catered to her mistress' needs, who licked her mistress' pussy! Screw those other ones, she thought, that one who is still a rookie, and especially that one who needs her skin flayed off! Imagine acting that way toward the mistress! Brenda would have liked to whip that insolent bitch herself, for not treating Mistress Wendy with the proper respect. But then she laughed to herself. All those bitches had to put their clothes on and go home by themselves, while she was left behind in her mistress' house to serve and obey the teacher!

Wendy's thoughts were on the classroom as well. Her mind's eye saw Margot bent over the padded horse with her strong wrists and shapely ankles firmly fettered to the unforgiving steel rings. How deliciously creamy her skin looked! And how much better it was when it welled up red and bloody after the taste of the lash! Her clit throbbed, and when Brenda's tongue flicked over it, she shivered with the mad hot rush through her body. Again she could see the whip rise and fall on that vulnerable skin. She could see the thin lines of blood appear, mingled with sweat, along the sides of each hideous welt. And those words, rushing out between sobs: "Please, Mistress, mercy!" The cunt had begged for mercy! And Wendy had simply smiled and brought the lash down again. That face, that face that had been so sullen and so proud, now streaming with tears and swollen from crying, and that look in her eyes that told Wendy that they both knew who had been the victor. The whole scene made Wendy so hot, her skin seemed alive and pulsating. "Lick me, slave!" she ordered, and then stretched out to enjoy the results.

Brenda did as she was told. She ran her fingernails up and down the insides of Wendy's thighs, then applied her tongue hard against the side of Wendy's clit before moving up and down the length of her pussy in slow, graceful sweeps. She circled Wendy's tight asshole and played over it with the very tip of her tongue, then moved back up to circle the hole to her hot tunnel before moving further up to tongue her clit.

Wendy's hands were on her nipples, which poked through the holes in her leather bra so invitingly. She kneaded and pulled at them, amazed at how hard and long they had become. It was a combination of Brenda's tongue in her cunt and the thought of how she had beaten Margot into a sniveling, pleading slave that made them hard, and she pinched them and dreamed up further punishments.

The hot wave crept up on her so quickly she could hardly believe it. Brenda teased her clit back and forth, then sucked on it, rubbing it with the tip of her tongue as she held it between her lips. Within moments, Wendy felt her cunt grow hot, and then her belly was on fire. The orgasm swept through her as

Brenda kept her mouth firmly on her mistress' pussy, sucking until every last thrill was spent.

"Enough, slave," Wendy said, and Brenda sat back on her heels, waiting for her next command. It came when Wendy rolled over onto her stomach. "Massage my back," she said.

Carefully Brenda unhooked the leather bra, then swiftly got up and rushed to the closet, returning with a bottle of expensive perfumed lotion. She squirted a wide squiggle of it on Wendy's back, then began to rub it in. Wendy relaxed under her hands. Since that first disastrous foot massage that had helped to bring about the whole idea of the slavery school, Wendy had given her slave books on the art of massage. She still wasn't an expert masseuse, but she had learned well enough that her movements on Wendy's back were enjoyable.

When the lotion had been worked in and Wendy felt no more tension in her muscles, she ordered Brenda to run her a hot bath. Again the blonde slave obeyed so quickly that Wendy had to secretly smile. Her fellow dominatrixs weren't the only ones benefitting from the classes!

The bath was ready shortly. As she had been taught, Brenda regulated the temperature with a bath thermometer, then added her mistress' favorite oils to the water before announcing that the tub was ready. To her extreme joy, she was allowed the privilege of helping her mistress out of her leather garter, boots, and stockings.

Wendy let out a little sigh of delight as she lowered herself into the steamy water. This was what being a mistress was all about! Her pussy eaten with a simple command, her back massaged, her bath drawn for her, and all she had to do was lie back and enjoy it.

She relaxed for a long time, until the water finally began to cool down. She was sleepy now, and called for Brenda to bring her a towel. Brenda appeared immediately, with a huge fluffy bath towel. As Brenda wrapped it around her, Wendy was pleased to note that it had been warmed for her. Her little slave, so rough and filled with bad habits, was rapidly turning into a submissive she could be proud to own.

Brenda held a satin robe open for her, then rushed to the kitchen to put on some boiling water for the tea her mistress had ordered. She served it to Wendy, who was lounging on the sofa reading a magazine, and sat quietly at her mistress' feet on the floor while Wendy finished both her reading and her hot drink.

"I'm going to bed now, slave," she said, and Brenda was disappointed, expecting to be told to leave. She perked up immediately when Wendy added, "I have an early appointment and I want my breakfast and coffee brought to me before I leave. You'll have to stay here tonight; I can't be bothered getting up to let you in that early."

Brenda's heart rose, and she whispered, "Thank you, Mistress!" quickly and sincerely. She knew it meant sleeping on the hardwood floor outside of Wendy's door, and she knew just how stiff and uncomfortable she was going to be in the morning. But she didn't care; she was staying with her mistress!

Wendy wasn't giving her slave a bit of thought, however. Her mind was on the morning. She had a couple of things to clear up at the office—might as well go in, she thought, I can leave when I have to—and then she planned on stopped by Julie's boutique and asking about a couple of chastity belts. They looked so interesting, and Wendy was sure she could find a use for them. Then, at noon, she had arranged lunch with Diane and Leah, to discuss how the school was going and how their slaves were behaving. She had also phoned Anne, who wanted to meet her and discuss how Leslie's schooling was progressing, but Wendy had been careful not to make any plans for the afternoon. A lunch with Diane and Leah could lead to just about anything, and Wendy wanted to keep her options open.

She went into the bedroom and slipped between the cool sheets. Brenda tucked in the blankets at the foot of the bed, then turned out the light and closed the door behind her. She went through the house and turned off all the lights, then returned to the door behind which her beloved mistress was sleeping.

She took a moment to finger the heavy leather collar still around her neck, then she kissed the fingers that had touched it, and curled up into a ball on the cold hardwood floor. It was the best bed she could have imagined and within moments she fell into a deep sleep filled with dreams of her tall, dark, leather-clad mistress.

SEVEN

"Chastity belts?" Julie said. "Wendy, you won't believe this. I think you are psychic." She disappeared into the back room.

Wendy spent her time looking over the marvelous collection that hung from the walls of Julie's store. It was erotic just being in here, surrounded by all the tools of her trade in all their diversity. She hoped that Julie would be gone for a while so that she could just stand there and enjoy. She closed her eyes and breathed deeply. The musky smell of leather was sweeter than the most expensive perfume.

She walked over and fingered a lovely thick braided whip. She could feel the muscles in her arm tighten as she imagined a lovely slave, desperately in need of punishment, bent over her padded horse, waiting for the first blow to land. The sound such a whip would make as it whistled through the air! And the snap it would make as it landed on that fair, untouched skin! She could see the welt rise, hear the slave sob. Her pussy was stirring deliciously as she walked over and looked at a mask.

This one was leather, made to cover a slave's head, with small holes so that she would be able to breathe and see. She had one at home that she had yet to use; she was waiting for the day when a slave would do something bad enough to deserve it. She didn't want to use it for some petty indiscretion; this was going to be a special treat, for slave and mistress both. She played with the heavy chrome zipper that closed the hole for the mouth. It was going to be a fantastic day when it finally arrived, she decided.

She spent some time examining several paddles, fashioned from leather and rubber, some with holes in their faces, some with studs. She liked paddles, liked the heavy, direct blows she could give with them. Unlike whips, she could feel the slaps of the paddle right through her arm, and they covered such a wide expanse of a naughty slave's skin. They were a treat to use and she could always reduce a haughty slave to tears with just a few well-placed strikes.

Julie came out of the back room carrying items wrapped in plastic bags. "I got them in just yesterday," she said. "I didn't even have time to unpack them, which is why I don't have any on display yet."

She opened one bag. The belt was an amazing thing, fashioned out of hard, cold chrome and warm, thick leather straps. Like the one Wendy had seen in the film, they were cleverly made so that a slave could wear them at all times, even when using the toilet, but there was no possibility of sexual contact. They closed with a small lock and tiny key, ensuring that only the person who placed it on the slave could remove it again. The slave would be helpless, trapped in the unyielding device until her mistress finally decided it could be removed. Wendy was amazed by their beauty and by the way they were exciting her. She would have complete sexual control over her slaves even when they were miles away from her.

"They are nice, aren't they?" Julie said. "My supplier brought them to my attention and, of course, I just had to order a few. I really think they're going to be hot sellers."

"They are now," Wendy said, fingering the leather straps. "I'll take two of them. That should do me for now. And by the way, what do you have in the way of nipple clamps?"

Julie showed her a selection, and when Wendy was finished, she once again had a large shopping bag filled with several different devices, all intended to keep her students in line.

"Did you give Elizabeth a call?" Julie asked, writing out the bill for Wendy's purchases. "You know, the woman I recommended?"

"That very day," Wendy said. "I went to see her, and you were right. She's exactly what I was looking for. Right now she's working on the items I asked her to make up. They'll be ready for the day that my students graduate."

"Your students are going to be the envy of everyone," Julie said. "Not only will they be perfectly trained, but they'll be wearing those! You're going to have mistresses banging your door down, begging you to take their slaves into your school."

"Well, I'm going to be limiting my classes to five slaves at a time," Wendy said. "That's the number I find best to work with. I do hope I have more to fill up my class when these are through. It really tears me apart! One side of me is looking forward to turning out perfectly trained slaves and being able to say that I taught them how to behave. The other side of me is dreading it, because it's so much fun commanding all five of them at once."

"Well, when your own slave graduates, you have to bring her here and let me have a look," Julie said. "I really want to see how those little goodies look."

"I will," Wendy said, and picked up her well-filled shopping bag. "I promise. I'm looking forward to seeing her with one myself."

Outside, she got into her Lincoln and drove to the restaurant where she was to meet Diane and Leah. Once again she was early, and she sat at a table and ordered a drink while she waited. The waiter brought her a glass, and Wendy was thrilled when she noticed how closely the actions of her students matched his graceful, fluid motions. In such a short time she had brought her charges so much closer to perfection.

Diane appeared shortly afterward, and Leah came in just a few minutes later. They greeted each other with quick kisses, then sat down and ordered cocktails. Leah's eyes were shining with excitement.

"Wendy!" she said. "You are a marvel! How on earth did you do it?"

"Do what?" Wendy asked, puzzled.

"Margot, my bitch!" she said. "I ordered her to come over last night after her class was finished. She came over right away, with no argument at all. She obeyed every command—just a little slowly, but nothing like before—and didn't question anything. I couldn't believe it was the same slave!"

Wendy smiled. "You looked at her back, didn't you?"

Leah closed her eyes. "It was magnificent." She turned to Diane. "You just wouldn't believe it, Diane.

Whip marks like railroad tracks all over her back. They'd been bleeding a bit, it was still on her shirt. They were just gorgeous. I got so excited I made her pleasure me, and she actually did an adequate job."

"With Margot, it's going to be quality of lessons, not so much quantity," Wendy said, basking in the glow of her success. "She's got to be outsmarted. I put her in positions where she expected to be punished, but she got nothing. That confused her. Then when she thought that was going to be my method, I bent her over my horse and beat the shit out of her."

"Brilliant," Diane said as she sipped her drink.

"Oh, the battle's not over yet," Wendy cautioned. "I'm not resting on my laurels, because I know I haven't completely won. She's still got a streak in her that she has to lose before I can even begin to think about graduating her. But I think she knows that ultimately I will win. It's just a question of how long it takes for me to do it."

"Well, your methods are fantastic," Leah raved. "Even her wrists and ankles were raw where you'd chained her up. It was beautiful."

"You are doing a fine job, Wendy," Diane agreed. "I can see the change in Alicia already. And even Anne was going on about how much you've taught her little novice." She smiled. "And you said it wouldn't work! You should have listened to me right from the very beginning. I knew you'd be the best possible person for the job."

Wendy smiled modestly. "Well, I think you're both going to be happy when your slaves graduate," she said. "They'll be trained to the very best of my ability. And they'll have their special graduation honors, which I'm sure you're going to love."

"Still won't give us a hint, will you?" Diane said.

"Not one," Wendy teased. "But believe me,

graduation day is going to be enjoyed by everyone."

The waiter came by and took their orders. Their lunch, when it arrived, was excellent; afterward they sat with cups of hot coffee and small snifters of fine brandy on the side.

It was obvious that Leah's mind was far away, and Diane teased her about her inattention.

"I'm really sorry," she said, flushed with embarrassment. "My mind was elsewhere, I guess."

"Worried about something?" Diane asked.

"Oh, no!" Leah said. "I was thinking about the way Margot looked when she came in last night. You could see submission in her eyes, and her wrists were all chafed and raw. Then I ordered her to strip, and she did it, right away. Then I saw her back—oh, Diane, you wouldn't believe what Wendy did whipping her. I'm getting hot and wet just seeing it all over again."

"I can understand that," Diane said, smiling seductively. "I've been looking at Wendy's beautiful new dress while we've been sitting here. It sure fits nice around those beautiful tits of yours, Wendy. I could lift them out and suck on them right here and now."

Wendy picked up her snifter and drained it. "That's enough out of both of you," she said. "I've been teased enough. Either you're both going to be quiet, or you're going to put your words into actions. In or out?"

"In, of course!" Diane laughed, and she and Leah quickly finished their coffee. Wendy called for the check and set down a credit card while the others gathered their belongings.

Outside, they got into Wendy's Lincoln and she drove them toward Leah's apartment. The sexual tension inside the car was almost strong enough to touch, and Wendy thought her panties would be soaked right through to her skirt before they arrived. Her nipples were hard and pressed against her shirt. She looked over at Diane, who sat in the front seat beside her; she could see that the tall, thin black woman was ever so carefully squirming in her seat, trying to appease her throbbing pussy.

The valet took the car and the doorman opened the doors for them at Leah's building. Once upstairs, Wendy got a surprise when Leah opened the door to her apartment: Ellen, naked except for the lather collar that identified her as Wendy's student, sat on the carpet. A chain snapped to the collar held her securely to the sofa. The little slave put her eyes down respectfully as the three mistresses entered the room.

"Good afternoon, Ellen," Leah said, as she threw her thin coat on the chair.

"Good afternoon, Mistress," Ellen said, then added, "Good afternoon, Mistress Wendy; good afternoon, Mistress Diane."

"Nice touch," Diane complemented Leah.

"She's been there since I ordered her over early this morning," Leah said. "Don't worry, Wendy, she'll be at your next class. I just felt like having her around today." She turned to the small woman shackled to the sofa. "Do you have to use the washroom, slave?" she asked.

"Yes, Mistress," Ellen replied. "Very badly, Mistress."

"Good," Leah said, and led the other two women into the bedroom. "You can wait until I'm ready, and be aware of what will happen if you stain the carpet." She closed the bedroom door, and Ellen hung her head, straining desperately for sounds through the bedroom door, wishing desperately that she could be permitted to serve all three mistresses at once.

Leah, of course, forgot Ellen completely once she closed the door. Her mind was focused entirely on the two beautiful women who were now hugging each other and kissing deeply. "Make room for one more," she laughed, and the three stood together, kissing back and forth, without regard to whose mouth they were kissing so long as they had lips to meet and a tongue to touch with their own.

It was Leah who first unbuttoned her blouse, and then suddenly they were all struck with a desire to undress. Within moments, their horrendously expensive designer clothes were simply piles on the floor, and their beautiful breasts and dark pussies turned them on even more. Now they were massaging nipples and slipping hands between legs, again without regard as to who they were touching so long as their hands were full.

Diane took the initiative, and pulled away toward the bed. "Come here, my honeys," she crooned. "I want to taste pussies, so don't take forever." Wendy and Leah were kissing deeply and holding each other's nipples, squeezing and pulling them gently, but they broke apart and moved toward the gorgeous black body that was now stretched out on the huge bed.

It was Wendy who got on her knees and put her pussy over Diane's probing tongue. Meanwhile, Leah got between her legs and gently pushed her thighs apart. "Such a gorgeous hot pussy!" she crooned, and within moments she was down on the bed, her mouth firmly on Diane's ruby red cunt lips. Diane moaned gently as Leah's hot tongue touched her clit, and she grabbed Wendy's asscheeks and pulled them down so that she could force her own tongue into the burning hot beauty of Wendy's pussy.

Within moments, the three of them were moaning as they licked and sucked each other. Wendy, with Diane's tongue lashing over her clit, reached down and stroked Diane's tits, then tweaked the hard nipples. Diane responded by pushing her tongue into Wendy's hole.

Leah, meanwhile, was taking her own sweet time on Diane's delicious cunt. She licked the smooth, dark thighs, then moved up to tickle the tightly curled hair over Diane's mound. Her fingers lightly touched Diane's pussy lips, followed by the very tip of her tongue. She moved all around the clit carefully, licking with long, slow strokes.

All the time her other hand was in her own cunt, moving over her clit with gently rocking motions that sent sweet shivers throughout her body. Her moans were whispery as she licked Diane's wet cunt and fingered her own juicy lips.

Outside the door, chained to the sofa, Ellen could hear the muffled moans of the three mistresses as they enjoyed each other. She held her breath, listening, imagining the wonderful scene inside. The throbbing heat in her pussy was tempered with the agony of a bladder filled to bursting and begging to be released. She could only sit, not daring to touch herself, and hope that when they were finished she would be ordered to bring them drinks, or help them to dress—anything for these gorgeous women who were her superiors!

Wendy, perched on Diane's tongue, her hands all over her dark magnificent breasts, looked down at Leah. "Oh, hon," she said, "you can't be getting yourself off! This is supposed to be treats for everyone."

Diane stooped for a moment. "All by herself?" she asked. "Oh, that won't do at all. Here, Wendy, move around so that we can all get a turn."

Wendy did, lying on the bed beside Diane, turned so that her hot pussy was close enough for Diane to lick. Leah moved up as well, and the three of them formed a chain. Within seconds they were licking each other again; Wendy's tongue was firmly in Leah's cunt, while Leah was once again eating Diane, and Diane lapped at Wendy.

"Much better," Wendy crooned, and gave her attention over to Leah's dark-haired pussy. Although she dearly loved lying back and ordering a slave to pleasure her, Wendy also loved having her tongue in another mistress' pussy, and she ate Leah with practiced strokes that soon had Leah moaning and bucking her hips.

All three of them were becoming more and more turned on as they licked and were licked in turn. Their moans were louder, and each woman was trying to grind her pussy hard against the tongue that was giving her so much pleasure. The sweet, thick smell of sex hung in the air and filled each woman's nose as the hot nectar filled their mouths. The only thing on Wendy's mind was the hot clit she was licking and the shivery rush that coursed through her body from Diane's tongue.

Not only their tongues were busy, but their hands were everywhere, caressing skin, squeezing asscheeks and pinching nipples. Ellen, listening to their wild moaning through the wall, savored the sounds, shivered at the unique sensation of her hot pussy and her painful bladder, and hooked two fingers through her heavy leather collar, rubbing it as gently and lovingly as if it were a mistress' body.

Diane stopped suddenly and lifted her head from Wendy's cunt. "Let's play switch," she suggested, and the other two stopped and turned around on the bed. The chain was reversed; Diane was now enjoying

Leah, Leah was licking Wendy, and Wendy's tongue found the ruby richness of Diane's hot cunt.

"Oh, right there," Wendy groaned, as Leah's tongue found its mark on Wendy's clit. She then applied herself fully to Diane, running up and down the familiar folds of skin and into the hot depths of her wet treasure.

Leah was enjoying some very intense sensations of her own, and Diane moaned enthusiastically as Leah pressed her cunt hard against the tongue that was doing its magic on her. She stiffened, then gasped and moved her hips frantically. Her tongue never left Wendy's pussy, but she cried out and trembled all over as she came.

"First one out!" Diane laughed, picking up on an old game they had often played. Like a loser in musical chairs, Leah moved aside on the bed while Wendy and Diane maneuvered into a sweet sixty-nine. There was no shame in losing at this game, however, and Leah was quick to join in on the other two, squeezing Wendy's firm, creamy asscheeks and reaching between the two to fondle Diane's delicious tits.

The two dominatrixs ate each other with a delicate fury, their tongues whipping over each other at a speed that seemed almost impossible to achieve. Turned on as they were, they seemed capable of licking each other for hours like that. Both were moaning as they lapped up pussy juice.

Diane softly whimpered as she could feel her pussy tighten and heat up. Wendy kept up the pressure on her hot nub, and very shortly Diane was also crying out and thrashing on the bed as her orgasm swept over her. Her skin was glistening with sweat and she hugged Wendy tightly as she came.

Wendy had been on the bottom, and she stretched out as Diane moved down on the bed. "I won this one!" she laughed, as Diane tried to catch her breath.

"It's not over yet," Diane said, as she and Leah moved on the bed. Leah pushed Wendy onto her side and then, before Wendy even realized what was happening, they were both licking her, Leah from the front and Diane from behind. Wendy gasped. To be licked by one beautiful woman was fantastic, but from both sides by two—heavenly!

Diane and Leah were both getting into their work, and their tongues mingled together over Wendy's pussy. This was a new experience for all three of them and they were enjoying it immensely. Wendy felt like her whole pussy was being covered by their probing tongues, and Leah's hands tweaking her nipples just added to her ecstasy.

"Oh, that's so good," Wendy crooned, and she arched her back and pushed her cunt hard against the two tongues that worked her over so expertly. Her whole body was tingling and she felt almost light-headed from the wild sensations that were rushing from her pussy. If there's a heaven, she thought, it has to be pretty close to this.

Leah was now sucking on her clit, and Diane's long tongue was probing deep inside her hot tunnel. Wendy could feel the hot pressure building up in her belly and she cried, "Harder! Please!" The two women pushed their tongues against her fiery wetness and flashed over her clit.

"Oh, keep that up!" she cried, as Leah's tongue pushed her clit back and forth and Diane probed at her hole. They did, and it wasn't long before the rich sensation swept over Wendy completely. She moaned and gasped, and the two women rode out her orgasm, their tongues flashing over her until she was completely spent.

"So, Wendy," Diane teased, as Wendy stretched out on the bed and enjoyed the afterglow of her orgasm, "is it true that two are better than one?"

"Well, that one really had a lot to recommend it," Wendy smiled. "Come here, both of you." They lay down on each side of her and Wendy kissed each of them as they hugged each other. She loved the taste of her own pussy on their mouths and she pressed her tongue in deeply to enjoy it.

They stayed locked in each other's arms for a long time. Wendy couldn't believe how much the explosive orgasm had relaxed her, and she closed her eyes and just basked in being held tightly by her two gorgeous colleagues. If this was what happened, she thought, she would have to schedule meetings to discuss the students more often.

Eventually they got up, and Leah suggested that they go into the living room for coffee. They left their clothes on the floor and walked out of the bedroom.

Ellen looked up quickly, then dropped her eyes as the three came into the living room. She desperately wanted to stare at the three women, all of them naked, but she had been trained well enough that she focused her attention on the carpet, even when Leah came up behind her and unsnapped the chain that held her to the sofa. "Thank you, Mistress," she said.

"We will have coffee, Ellen," Leah ordered.

"Yes, Mistress," Ellen replied, getting up slowly. "Mistress, may I ask something?"

"Go ahead," Leah said.

"Mistress, please may I have permission to use the washroom?" Ellen's discomfort was very evident.

Leah turned her back and walked toward her favorite chair. "When I say you may," she said. "A little self-control is a very good thing."

"Yes, Mistress," Ellen replied, and went into the

kitchen. There were tears in her eyes and she prayed that her strained muscles would be able to hold out a little longer. It did not cross her mind to disobey the order. She had been told to wait, and wait she would, even if it meant squeezing her thighs together and concentrating everything she had on holding her muscles tight.

She brewed coffee and set out the cream and sugar, then arranged cups on a silver tray. Linen napkins and spoons were placed as Wendy had taught her. She then carried it into the living room and set it on the table before the three mistresses, with as deep a bow as she could manage with the agony of her full bladder.

"Wendy, I swear you've done miracles with this one, too," Leah said, as she took her cup of coffee. "I wasn't being served like this two weeks ago. You really are doing a fantastic job."

"Well, Ellen is doing well in her schooling," Wendy said, and she saw the small woman flush at the compliment. "I told you before, Leah, none of them will leave my school until they're perfect, and until they wear their honors."

"Still won't let it slip, will you?" Diane smiled.

"Not once," Wendy countered. "Just make sure you're there for the graduation ceremony and you'll see what I have up my sleeve. I guarantee you'll love it."

Leah sipped her coffee. "Our clothes must be all wrinkled up by now, lying on the floor," she said. "Ellen, go in and get our clothes and hang them up. Press them if they need it. When you're done you may use the washroom, but if I find you've hurried and done a poor job, then you'll think the punishment that Margot got from Mistress Wendy was a backrub!"

They ignored her as she rushed out of the room. Tears of shame were on Ellen's cheeks as she picked up the expensive clothes off the bedroom floor. Even her trips to the bathroom were regulated by her mistress! But her beloved mistress had ordered it, and Ellen would never consider anything but complete obedience. She got out the iron and carefully pressed out some stubborn wrinkles in the rich fabrics, then hung up everything on the lightly scented hangers from Leah's closet.

She checked each article minutely, making sure that there were no wrinkles left, and finally decided that they were as perfect as when the women had come in. She then rushed into the bathroom and sobbed with relief as she was finally able to empty her bladder.

The three women finished their coffee, and Wendy checked her book for Anne's number. She called and made an appointment to meet this woman whose slave was her student; Diane, who had introduced them, agreed to come along.

"Ellen, our clothes!" Leah called, and instantly Ellen appeared with them. Leah checked them for wrinkles, reminding Ellen of her threat should she find any. The little slave then helped Diane and Wendy to dress, holding their shoes for them and fastening buttons.

Diane and Wendy kissed Leah good-bye and waited while the valet brought the Lincoln to the door. They ignored his stare and got in.

"So what is Anne really like?" Wendy asked, as she drove toward the address she had been given over the phone.

Diane smiled, a little slyly. "I think you'll really like her, once you get to know her," she said. "You'll find she's a lot like us."

Anne's house turned out to be a huge one, with well-tended gardens, just on the outskirts of the city. As Wendy parked the Lincoln in the driveway, she noticed a young woman weeding a flower bed at the side of the house. She wondered if this gardener was a paid employee or, more likely, a slave happy to kneel in the dirt and plant flowers as her mistress had commanded.

The door was opened by Wendy's novice student, Leslie. She was surprised to see her teacher on the doorstep, but quickly composed herself and greeted them properly as she had been taught in school. Once they stepped inside, Leslie took their coats and then led them into the house.

Anne was waiting for them in the living room. Wendy was used to luxury, but even she was amazed at how gorgeous the house was. It was almost completely furnished with antique furniture, the mahogany polished until it shone like glass.

"Please sit down," Anne said, and Wendy and Diane enjoyed the comfort of the overstuffed sofa. "Leslie, some refreshments, please."

"Yes, Mistress," Leslie replied, bowing slightly before she hurried off down the hall.

"Diane, I can only thank you for telling me about Wendy's school," Anne said. "I've always taken on slaves who were set in their ways and it was almost impossible to train them to do things the way I wanted. Now I've not only started off with a novice, but she's being taught exactly the way she should be."

Wendy, meanwhile, was also grateful to Diane, for bringing her to Anne's house. Anne was irresistible. She was tall and slim, and her flawless skin was the same dark, rich tone as Diane's. Her clothes were exquisite, and her skirt was short enough that Wendy could admire her long, beautiful legs and high shoes. She could imagine Anne in tight leather, with a whip in her hands, and the thought was enough to make her pussy start throbbing again.

Leslie returned shortly carrying a silver tray with three wineglasses on it. Wendy sipped at hers and discovered a rich Chardonnay. She sat back on the sofa to enjoy both the wine and the company.

"How is the school working out overall, Wendy?" Anne asked, and Wendy thought she detected a special fire in the deep brown eyes.

"Better than I expected," Wendy replied. "I have to thank Diane as much as you do. After all, it was her idea."

"Any problems with discipline?" Wendy noticed an unmistakable look this time, and she knew instantly that under the sophisticated exterior, there was a cold and cruel mistress who thoroughly enjoyed the sound of a whip on flesh and the cries of a slave begging for mercy.

"Well, there's the usual little problems," Wendy admitted. "Your own slave needed a couple of taps now and again. I do have one that's actually thinking she can get the better of me and I'm having a lot of fun with her."

"Really?" Anne asked. "Actually thinks she's better than the teacher?"

"Well, she did at first," Wendy smiled. "Once I put her over a horse and laid her back open with a cat she got some second thoughts pretty quickly." Anne's eyes opened and Wendy knew she was imagining such a scene. Then she looked over at Diane, and saw her eyes close for a moment, then open wide. Poor Margot's punishment was being savored by both of them!

"That was enough to do it?" Anne asked, taking a drink of her wine.

"Well, my job's not quite done yet," Wendy said. "I have a few more tricks up my sleeve that I know will get this stupid notion out of her head. I'm waiting for the right time to use them. Besides," she added, "it's fun playing with her like this. She hasn't got a clue when the bomb's going to fall."

"And when it does?" Anne prompted, sitting on the very edge of her chair.

"When it does," Wendy promised, "she's going to be the sorriest slave I've ever seen."

"I wish I could be there to see it," Anne said huskily, sitting back and sipping her wine. "It sounds like a good time will be had by all."

"Anne has quite a few slaves here," Diane explained to Wendy.

"They're better than hired help!" Anne laughed. "They look after the yard and do the housework quite well and never ask for a raise. If they don't do everything just as they're supposed to, I have the pleasure of beating them. I had a slave specifically to attend to me, bring me meals, and run my bath, but she moved away and I replaced her with Leslie. I like the little slut, but she didn't know the first thing about serving me properly. That was why I was so glad to hear about your school, Wendy. You saved me the trouble of doing all that training myself, and now I just sit back and enjoy the results."

"I'm sure you will enjoy them," Wendy smiled. "Your slave is coming along very well. I have no doubt that she will graduate with honors soon."

"That reminds me," Anne said. "What is this graduation honor that I've heard so much about? Leslie mentioned it when I grilled her about the school, but she didn't seem to know much."

"No one does," Wendy said, "not even Diane. It's my little surprise for all of you, and I'm sure that you're going to be thrilled with it once your slave achieves it."

"Then she'd better learn her lessons and earn this surprise honor," Anne said. "If it's as interesting as your school, I'm sure I'll love it."

"Wendy's always full of surprises," Diane said. "I'm looking forward to this one too."

They finished their wine, and Wendy commented on how beautifully decorated the living room was.

"I really like antique furniture," Anne explained. "I've been collecting it for a number of years now. Would you like to see the rest of the house?"

"I certainly would," Wendy said, setting down her wineglass and standing up. As Anne stood up, Wendy admired her all over again. She had large, gorgeous breasts that were barely concealed under her low-cut blouse, and Wendy suddenly longed to put her tongue on that chocolately-smooth skin and reach for the nipples that she could glimpse as hard nubs under the silk fabric.

Anne took them on a tour of the house. As Wendy had suspected, the rest of the rooms were decorated in the same rich, luxurious style, the furniture hand-polished to a mirror finish, the rugs thick and comforting. The dining room could easily seat twelve, although Anne admitted that she lived alone, with regular visits from her slaves, who not only kept the house in perfect condition but also attended to their mistress whenever she required.

They went upstairs; Anne's bedroom contained a huge mahogany bed and matching antique furniture. Wendy noticed a leather paddle, its face studded with chrome nubs, on the bedside table. Her pussy grew warm as she looked at it, imagining Anne ordering a slave to lick her, and using the paddle hard on the slave's ass with each lap of the willing tongue.

"You keep your tools handy," she commented, as she walked around the bed and lightly brushed her fingers over the paddle.

"There are items in every room in the house," Anne said, smiling at her. "You just never know when you'll need something." She looked at Wendy, and the gleam in her eyes was obvious. "The slaves worry most when I'm in my library. That's where I keep my belts. I have a lovely one with sharp studs on it, which leaves a most beautiful impression on misbehaved slaves."

They left the bedroom and walked down the long hall, stopping before a door with an old-fashioned keyhole. "This is my special retreat," Anne said, fishing in her pocket for the key.

It turned out to be a special torture room. Smaller than Wendy's, but just as well stocked, it was a glorious tribute to the mistress' art. One wall was covered with steel rings for chaining slaves; another wall was covered with shelves and chests of drawers. The shelves were piled high with all manner of shackles, whips, handcuffs, collars, masks, and other goodies.

Wendy was examining the collection when she heard a sound behind her. She turned and was startled to find that a black shape in the corner was moving. She walked over and found that it was a slave, clad in a head-to-toe black rubber suit, complete with a mask with three holes for the victim's eyes and nose. The eyes that looked out at her contained that intoxicating mixture of fear and delight. Around the rubber-clad throat was a stiff rubber collar, attached to the wall by a short, thick metal chain.

"What happened here?" Wendy asked. The other two turned around; Diane was also startled, then intrigued by the rubber-clad slave who sat, curled into a ball, on the hard floor.

"My kitchen wench," Anne explained. "Just a little while before you came, we had an episode with the dish washing. It seems that one of the crystal wineglasses slipped, or so the story goes, and smashed on the floor. This is her reward for that so-called slip."

"It looks terribly uncomfortable," Wendy observed.

"I would imagine that it is," Anne said. "I have to be carefully, since I've had a few pass out after a while. The rubber really is effective, though. I don't think I've ever had to use it twice for the same indiscretion."

She reached forward and grabbed the rubber mask at the back of the neck, then roughly tore it forward off the woman's face. The slave gasped and shook her head. Her short hair was plastered to her head with sweat, and her skin was mottled with a horrible reddish rash. She dared not speak a word.

"I've only used leather," Wendy said. "Maybe I should invest in one of these suits as well. It looks marvelous." It felt marvelous too, and her pussy was growing hotter and wetter the longer she looked at the slave, who had crumpled into a heap on the floor. Only the short length of chain at her throat kept her from falling over.

"We'll leave her for now," Anne said, as Diane and Wendy followed her out of the room and watched as she locked the door again. Wendy could imagine the slave's horror at once again hearing the key turn in the lock. "That one can take a lot of punishment, and after all, it *was* one of the nicer glasses."

They glanced into the huge bathroom, with its sunken tub, gold fixtures, and marble sinks. They were about to move on when Wendy noticed a glass door inside. "Where does that go to?" she asked.

"I'll show you," Anne said, and led them over to it. It opened into a large room, its walls lined with cedar; in the center was a whirlpool.

"Very nice," Diane said.

"You know, that's something I've often thought about getting in my own house," Wendy said. "I've only used the one at the health club. Are they really all that nice?"

"Well, don't take my word for it," Anne smiled. "We can try it out if you like."

"I didn't bring a bathing suit," Wendy said, not quite sure of her hostess' intentions.

"I was sort of hoping you didn't," Anne said.

Diane smiled at Wendy over Anne's shoulder, commenting, "See, I told you she was just like us."

Wendy was so eager she could hardly believe herself. Anne pushed a small button on the wall by the whirlpool; within moments, Leslie was at the door. "Some towels and refreshments," Anne ordered, and Leslie disappeared to fulfill her mistress' command.

Anne began to undress, and Diane and Wendy unbuttoned their clothes as well. To Wendy's delight, Anne was just as lovely as she had imagined. Her breasts were soft and full and her nipples were huge; Wendy could see herself sucking on them.

Anne reached for Diane, and within moments the two were in each other's arms. Wendy watched them as they kissed slowly, their tongues in each other's mouths, their hands caressing smooth skin and hard nipples. Then Diane broke off the kiss.

"Wendy, come here," she said. "Don't let us have all the fun." Wendy stepped over to them and within seconds she was into her second threesome of the day, her hands reaching for breasts and pussies as the soft dark hands reached for her own.

The three were still kissing when Leslie tiptoed in with their towels and drinks. Setting them quietly beside the whirlpool tub, she wondered whether or not to disturb them and announce that she had brought everything. She decided against it and stepped back out of the room.

She was intrigued by the three dominatrixs, embracing, kissing and fondling each other, and she stopped for a second. Perhaps if she stood just outside the door they wouldn't realize she was there. She thought about it for a moment, and then remembered Lisa, the kitchen slave, who had been punished for dropping a wineglass. Anne had taken Leslie upstairs and shown her the poor slave, who had been clad in the fearsome rubber suit and left chained to the wall. The example was branded on Leslie's mind, and she knew that similar punishments would be selected for her if she were caught spying on the three. She turned and rushed from the bathroom.

"Let's get into the tub," Anne suggested, as she turned a dial on the wall. Instantly the water in the pool swirled into motion as the underwater jets, set into the pool's walls, shot the water out. The steaming, bubbling pool looked inviting, and Wendy stepped in and sat down.

What bliss! The hot water swirled all around her, and a jet right behind her back shot a massaging stream against her spine. She accepted the glass of wine that Anne offered her, taking a sip before putting her head back and closing her eyes. "Definitely," she said. "They can come in tomorrow and measure for one of these. I don't know how I ever got along without one."

"You won't be sorry," Anne promised, handing Diane a glass and then stepping into the bubbling waters herself. "Especially when I show you my little secret."

"What secret is that?" Diane asked, as she sipped at her wine and enjoyed the hot bubbling water.

"Watch," Anne said. She put down her wineglass and sat deep in the tub, facing the side of it. "Now you two do the same thing."

Wendy set down her drink, mystified, and assumed a similar position. As soon as she faced the tub wall she understood. What a secret! The jet that had been forcing hot water on her back was now shooting a deliciously hard stream of water right at her pussy.

Diane had found the right position as well. "Oh, Anne, you sly devil!" she said as the water rushed over her sensitive cunt. "No wonder you spend so much time in this thing!"

"Play with it like it's a vibrator," Anne suggested.

Wendy did. By raising herself off the bottom of the tub, she could control how the torrent of water pressed against her. She sat right up against the jet, letting the water play over the entrance to her hole and push against the tight bud of her ass. Then she moved down, and the cascade sent shivers through her as the water pushed her clit.

Anne turned a chrome knob on the side of the tub, and instantly the bubbles in the water increased so that they gently tickled the women's nipples when they broke against them. Wendy moaned softly at this combination of a gentle caress on her tits and the firm spurt of water on her cunt, and she closed her eyes and enjoyed the hot rushes that went through her whole body. She felt almost weightless in the water; her pussy seemed to float up to meet the spray as it coursed out of the underwater jet.

"Anne, this is positively divine," Wendy said, feeling her body tighten up in response to the spurt of water on her clit.

"Let me make it even better for you then," Anne said. She slipped over beside Wendy and put her hand down between Wendy's legs. Her fingers found Wendy's pussy. Gently she pulled the pussy lips wide open so that Wendy's clit was completely exposed to the jet of water.

"Oooooh!" Wendy moaned as the water rushed directly onto her. With her other hand, Anne found Diane's pussy and held it open as well to the relentless surge.

"That's as good as a tongue on it!" Wendy moaned, moving her hips and working her pussy all around the jet. "Hold it open, Anne! Wider!"

Her fingers were now on her nipples, squeezing and tweaking them. Her whole body was alive to the sensations from her tits and her pussy. She leaned back and met Anne's mouth in a rich, deep kiss. The feeling of Anne's hot tongue against her own only added to her delight. They broke off and Anne turned to kiss Diane the same way, then she returned to Wendy. Back and forth their kisses went as Anne held both their pussies open, and Diane and Wendy played with their nipples in the steamy whirlpool.

Wendy played the jet like a lover, moving closer to it, then back, up and down, experiencing the full range of sensations on her pussy. Anne's hand followed every movement. Wendy's heart was racing and she could feel the buildup all through her body when she finally concentrated the stream right on her rock-hard clit. She gasped as her body, already hot from the steamy water, burned with a special fire all its own.

"Kiss me!" Wendy demanded, and Anne turned to press hard against her lips. Wendy's tongue lashed as the hot rush from her pussy grew in intensity, spreading throughout her belly and up through her whole body. She thrashed against the torrent of water as she came, moaning, her mouth locked on Anne's, her body trembling, her fingers grabbing her rock-hard nipples.

She was just about to relax when Anne, with a smile, pressed her fingers against Wendy's clit, holding her pussy lips open again to the jet. Within seconds, her clit responded and she groaned as her whole pussy throbbed and burned. A second orgasm, even stronger than the first, ripped through her and she cried out.

"Now you can sit back," Anne laughed, and Wendy collapsed against the side of the tub, gasping, while Anne worked her magic on Diane. Within a few moments, Diane was also gasping and crying out as she came.

Not to be outdone, Anne finally concentrated on her own pleasure, and sat as the jets played their familiar dance on her clit. She moaned and trembled as her orgasm rocked her, and finally she too relaxed and sat back with the others.

Once again, they hugged and traded kisses as the swirling hot water bubbled up around them. Wendy enjoyed a drink of her cold wine and sat back to enjoy the massage.

"That's some secret, Anne," she said, as her breathing gradually returned to normal. "That was one of the best ones I've ever had."

"It does create some pretty intense ones," Anne agreed, sipping her drink. "A lot of people say a whirlpool really relaxes you. I don't think they realize just how true that is."

Diane smiled mischievously. "Any more little secrets, Anne?"

"I've got a whole bag of tricks," Anne smiled. She rang the buzzer beside the pool; in a moment, Leslie appeared at the door.

"Slave, tell the kitchen that there will be two guests for dinner," Anne said. "Then come back here and prepare robes and towels for us. We will have cocktails in the living room before dinner."

"Yes, Mistress," Leslie said, and turned to go.

"One more thing, slave!" Anne said.

"Mistress?" Leslie asked.

"When you return," Anne said, "be sure you are naked, with just a collar around your throat." She smiled at Diane and Wendy. "We might like a little after-dinner entertainment."

EIGHT

"Mistress, please!" Alicia begged. "No, Mistress! Please have mercy!"

"I am merciful, worm," Wendy replied. "I could have chained you upside down."

Alicia sobbed. She stood spread-eagled, chained by her wrists and ankles to the X-frame against the wall. Her bare back was exposed to her teacher, who stepped behind her with a varnished wooden paddle in her hand.

The other four students were kneeling on the floor, watching; Margot's eyes were bright with anticipation. Alicia had committed the grievous error of being one minute late for class.

"This will be a lesson to all of you," Wendy said. She walked back and forth between the students on the floor and the black-haired woman chained to the frame, her shoes tapping a warning on the hard wood. Her costume this day was a body-hugging catsuit made of supple black leather. "Punctuality is one of the most important things a slave must learn. If she is not punctual, she is not obedient. If she is not obedient, then she will never be a perfect slave."

She reached over and ran the wooden paddle down Alicia's spine and into the crack of her delicate ass. Alicia held her breath. When the paddle was removed, she let out a sob.

"Imagine this picture," Wendy said. "Your mistress tells you to meet her outside a restaurant at five o'clock. You don't arrive until a quarter past. Your mistress stands outside for fifteen minutes waiting for you. She looks foolish hanging around outside a restaurant waiting. People wait for her, she doesn't wait for them! Would you put your mistress in such a situation?"

She waited; the slaves were silent. Wendy whacked the paddle against her palm with a loud crack. "Would you?" she demanded.

"No, Mistress!" the class chimed.

"Late is late," Wendy said. "Whether it's one minute or fifteen, it's still disobedience. And it will not be tolerated!"

Thwack! The wooden paddle landed on Alicia's buttocks. She cried out, and the other slaves winced. The long, thin paddle left a stunning welt across both asscheeks. Wendy smiled with satisfaction.

"If your mistress tells you to arrive at five, you arrive at five o'clock," Wendy continued. "You are not early, you are not late. You are precisely punctual."

Thwack! Another welt joined the first on Alicia's creamy asscheeks. Her face was wet with tears and she slumped against the frame, held up by the shackles on her wrists.

"You do not try to outthink your mistress, and you do not try to anticipate her," Wendy continued. "You do exactly what you are told. If she says five o'clock, you are there at exactly five o'clock. If you know she is going to be late, you are there at five o'clock, and you wait for her. There is no other way to behave."

Thwack! Thwack! The blows came quickly together, and Alicia gritted her teeth and squeezed her eyes shut to keep from screaming out. Her ass was burning and blood red.

"That looks so nice," Wendy said, standing back and admiring her handiwork. "I hope this is an effective lesson for all of you. If anyone is late for any other class, she will not graduate. Period." Thwack! "She will not participate in the graduation ceremony, and she will not receive her graduation honor." Thwack! "She will have to repeat her lessons, and be shamed before all of her classmates and her mistress." Wendy held the paddle with both hands now, and delivered a final, terrifyingly hard blow to Alicia's ass. Alicia screamed, then sobbed loudly as her poor bruised ass welled up an angry red in response.

Wendy put the paddle down and went back to the front of the classroom. "Does everyone understand?" she asked.

"Yes, Mistress," the class replied.

"I would suggest that before you leave today, you ensure that your watches are synchronized with the clock here," she said, ignoring Alicia's loud sobs. "It might help you avoid the situation your poor sister has gotten herself into."

Wendy then went on with her regular lesson, teaching the slaves how to make and serve coffee. She noticed that every now and again, Margot stole a quick glance over at Alicia as she hung on the X-frame, her buttocks raw and burning. Wendy couldn't mistake the look in Margot's eyes, and she knew that the tall gorgeous slave longed to be paddled herself.

"Margot," Wendy said, "perhaps you'd like to demonstrate to the rest of the class how to set the tray for coffee."

Margot paused just a moment before she replied, "Yes, Mistress," and Wendy knew that she was eager for her share of punishment. She was definitely jealous that Alicia had received such cruel fare and when she got up, she walked slowly. From the corner of her eye, she watched Wendy to see if her tardiness was having any effect.

If it was, Wendy didn't let it show. She played Margot as she had before, teasing her with a promise of pain and then holding back. She picked up a riding crop and used it to gently tap Margot's hand, explaining that she should pick up the cup by the handle. Margot left her hand on the cup for a moment longer, then realized that there would be no further blows from the crop. Disappointed, she handled the cup properly and put it on the tray.

"The napkin must be folded properly," Wendy said, and the class watched as Margot folded it. The spoon was placed incorrectly, but again to her disappointment, Margot received only a slight tap with the riding crop as a warning.

The rest of the class looked on, wondering why Wendy wasn't beating this slave senseless. A sharp glance from their mistress immediately let them know that such behavior would be tolerated from no one else. Kneeling on her heels, Brenda got the impression that the only person in the room who didn't realize a plan was brewing was Margot herself. The tall slave seemed oblivious to the fact that she was being set up for a terrible and final punishment. Brenda shivered involuntarily as she thought about what was going through her mistress' mind, and she was only grateful that her mistress' wrath would not be aimed at her.

The class watched as Margot poured the coffee into the cup and set it on the tray, then carried it over to Wendy and presented it.

"I trust everyone watched carefully," Wendy said, ignoring Margot who stood before her. Wendy then walked to the front of the class, leaving Margot standing foolishly in the middle of the room with the tray in her hands. Wendy watched from the corner of her eye.

Margot stood for a moment, almost in disbelief. She looked over at Wendy, who was now explaining the finer points of cappuccino to Brenda, Leslie and Ellen. She completely ignored Margot, whose face turned red. For a moment, Wendy thought that she might fling the tray to the floor. Instead, she stood for a long moment, then humbly brought the tray back to the front of the class. Still ignored by her mistress, she returned the tray to the table and then took her place beside the other three.

Another victory! Wendy thought triumphantly. Her plan was working, and the other slaves knew it too. It would only be a matter of time, and a few more events, before Margot would become the magnificent, perfectly trained slave that Wendy knew she could be. Leah was right; the slut was worth the trouble. Besides, Wendy was rather enjoying the cat-and-mouse game she was playing. The best part was that Margot seemed to be completely oblivious to it. The final showdown, Wendy knew, would be terrifying and also immensely satisfying. She was actually looking forward to it, even though an exact plan was still in the future.

Once they had gone over espresso and iced coffee, Wendy walked over to the wall and released the shackles on Alicia's wrists.

The young slave gasped in agony as the feeling came back into her numb hands as a prickly fire. She did not forget her training, however, and managed to sob, "Thank you, Mistress!" as she rubbed her chafed wrists. Her poor ass was still throbbing, colored a rich burgundy from the wooden paddle. Wendy noted that it would probably be a few days before she would be able to sit comfortably.

Wendy opened the cuffs that held her legs apart, then ordered Alicia over with the rest of the class. "Thank you, Mistress," Alicia repeated, as she hurried over to her place in line and knelt on the floor. Wendy noticed that while all the others sat on their heels, Alicia was careful to keep her asscheeks up so that the burnished skin would not be touched.

Wendy also noticed that Margot kept glancing over at Alicia. The fact that Alicia could not put her ass down was not lost on the tall, cold slave. Wendy decided that it was time to put Margot's longing for pain to good use. Although she hadn't planned on using this particular lesson just yet, it seemed like perfect timing. Not only would the other slaves benefit, but she would have an opportunity to win yet another victory over Leah's belligerent slave.

"You may recall," Wendy said, stepping to the front of the class, "that a little while ago, you were taught how to properly present yourselves when your mistress wanted to secure you. I believe we used such items as thumbscrews and handcuffs, did we not?"

"Yes, Mistress," the class chimed, and Wendy noticed that there was no hesitation on Margot's part when she answered.

"It's very important that your education be complete," Wendy continued. "The restraints we learned about the last time were very basic ones. It's time to move on to other things."

Margot's eyes went as bright as Christmas candles. As Wendy left the room, she saw that the tall slave followed her every move. When she returned, carrying a large bag, Margot looked like a child who had been promised candy. Keep falling, little one, Wendy thought. The trap is set and you're walking straight into it.

The first item Wendy pulled out of the bag was a bridle, her most recent acquisition from Julie's store. At the center was a cold steel snaffle bit, the same type that a horse would wear. The difference was that the leather bridle attached to it was shaped to go over a woman's head. There were long reins attached to the bit rings.

"Margot, come up here," Wendy ordered, and she marveled at how quickly Margot got up and rushed to the front of the classroom. Very soon, she thought, you'll be doing that for every command I give.

"The bridle is an important toy for a mistress," Wendy explained, holding it up. Margot's eyes never left it. "It can be used for riding a slave or for guiding her. It also makes a very good gag. Leslie, come up here."

Leslie did; Margot looked confused. Wendy turned to her. "Margot, put the bridle on Leslie," she said. "I think it's fairly obvious how it goes on."

Margot's face fell. She stood for a second, then replied, "Yes, Mistress," and unbuckled the straps to the bridle.

Leslie was totally unaware of Margot's disappointment; she was too excited by the bridle. As a novice, she had never seen such a thing, and she loved it. All the glasses of wine served, all the taps with the riding crop she had endured—now this was a reward! She could not believe how wet the device was making her pussy. She wanted to wear it for Mistress Wendy, and she longed to be buckled into it by her own beloved Mistress Anne.

She opened her mouth wide; Margot roughly shoved the bit in. The steel was cold on Leslie's tongue and it pinched painfully where the rings came out at the sides of her mouth, but, to her delight, she found that she loved it! Margot buckled the straps around her head and the bridle was firmly in place.

"On your knees," Wendy ordered, and Leslie did so eagerly. Wendy picked up a riding crop and grabbed the long reins, standing behind Leslie. She tapped Leslie's ass with the crop as she would a horse in harness. "Forward," she ordered. Leslie moved ahead on her hands and knees.

"You will notice how your mistress will use the bridle to control you," Wendy told the class. They were learning about this new form of control. But their lessons were nothing compared to the revelation that Leslie herself was going through.

She moved forward on her hands and knees in front of Mistress Wendy. As she did, her face flushed and her heart began beating wildly. She was so excited, she thought she might come just from Wendy pulling her head to the side with the bit. The smell of the leather, the steely taste of the bit in her mouth, even the coppery sting of the drop of blood that appeared at the corner of her lip—all excited her even more. So this was what being a slave was all about!

She had been controlled by her mistress through commands and through the occasional punishment she had received. But nothing compared to this! Mistress Wendy had total control over her. She slowed for just a moment, and received a sharp crack of the riding crop across her ass. She moved just slightly in the wrong direction, and had her head pulled back immediately by the reins. She could go nowhere on her own, do nothing that she wanted to do. She was completely in Mistress Wendy's control, at Mistress Wendy's mercy. And she loved it!

Wendy led her back to the front of the class. "Your mistress will undoubtedly come up with many more uses for this kind of device," she said. "A slave can also be ridden, in addition to being driven." To illustrate, she sat on Leslie's naked back.

Leslie gasped with pleasure. The weight on her back, the feel of Wendy's supple leather catsuit on her skin, the way Wendy gathered up the reins and used the ends to whip her across the shoulders—she shuddered and tightened the muscles in her pussy in an effort to stop it from throbbing so much.

Wendy ordered her forward, and Leslie immediately obeyed. It was much more difficult with the extra weight on her back, and at one point a tiny piece of gravel tracked in on Wendy's shoes cut painfully into her knee. She didn't care. She would have carried Wendy on her back out on the street if her teacher had ordered it. The only thing that could have made her happier at this point was if Mistress Anne had been there. But she was confident that her beautiful mistress would use this kind of treatment in the future. She would beg on her belly if necessary, but she would find a way to be controlled!

For her part, Wendy didn't miss any of Leslie's revelation. She had noticed the look in Leslie's eyes, heard her gasp and, most importantly, had seen the glint of moisture around Leslie's exposed pussy.

Wendy herself was so excited she could hardly believe it. She had succeeded! She knew exactly what Leslie was feeling at this point, and she knew why.

Wendy was so excited she could feel the crotch of her leather suit becoming hot and damp. She had taken an untrained, novice slave, who was so green she hardly even knew what slavery was all about, and had cultivated her from a tiny seed into a beautiful blossom.

Wendy rode Leslie around the room, and as ordered, the other slaves watched every move. One of them needed no orders to do so. Margot's mouth was positively watering as she watched. She glanced quickly into the large bag and saw a jumble of leather, chrome rings, and chains. She wondered what device she would be strapped into! Whatever it was, she would love it! She listened carefully as Wendy described how a slave should behave once she was strapped into the bridle. "Quite often you will be given a saddle to wear as well," she said, and both Margot and Leslie closed their eyes, letting a rush of sexual energy pass through them as they imagined the slap of the leather saddle as it was dropped on their backs and the heft of the metal stirrups slapping against their sides. Leslie longed for the feeling of the girth being tightened around her stomach, and she decided that as soon as she saw her Mistress Anne again, she would plead and beg for such treatment.

"Sometimes your mistress will even strap spurs on her boots," Wendy said, and Margot thought she might faint with the joy. Imagine the tips of blunt spurs against her ribs or, even better, a razor-sharp rowel! She could almost hear the jingle of the spurs and the ringing of their chains on the floor, how they would look against the black leather of a riding boot.

Her mind wandered to Mistress Leah, dressed in chaps and pointed-toe boots, spurs on them, fringed leather gloves on her hands, a riding whip between her fingers, carrying the saddle and bridle. How she would obey her commands then! How quickly she would drop to the floor when ordered! How she would carry her mistress around, speed up at the tap of a whip or the touch of a spur, change course when her head was cruelly pulled around by the bit! Her thighs were wet with juice as she imagined the scene, and both she and Leslie were disappointed when horse and rider returned to the front of the class and that portion of the lesson was finished.

Swiftly, Wendy unbuckled the bridle and pulled the bit out from between Leslie's teeth. "Face the class," she ordered, and Leslie did so. "Sit down there," she told Margot, indicating her spot in the lineup. Slowly, Margot left her spot beside the bag of leather devices and reluctantly knelt on the floor.

"Class, I believe that something very important has happened here right now," Wendy told the class. She looked down at Leslie. "Am I correct, slave?"

Leslie smiled, and tears of joy appeared at the corners of her eyes. "Oh, mistress, you know!" she beamed. "I was hoping you would, Mistress!"

Wendy smiled at her. "Perhaps you will tell the class what we're talking about," she said.

Leslie faced her classmates. "Mistress Wendy is correct," she said. "Something did happen just now. When my own mistress enrolled me in this school, I didn't really know a lot about being a slave. I thought it just meant that I would bring my mistress her wine when she asked for it, and rub her back when she ordered it, and carry out her duties. I'm ashamed to admit it," she said, lowering her head a little, "for a while I wasn't really sure if it was what I wanted. It seemed pretty menial to me. I didn't really understand why the other slaves my mistress kept always looked so happy and were so eager to serve my mistress. I knew I had to be missing the point of it all, but I didn't know exactly what the point was."

"Go on," Wendy coaxed. "Tell them what happened."

"It all became clear to me when Mistress Wendy put the bridle on me, and forced me to obey her," Leslie continued. "I'd never been controlled so physically before. I haven't been with my mistress very long and she hasn't had the time to restrain me and force me the way Mistress Wendy just did. Now I know what being a slave is all about. I don't have any will at all of my own. I am my mistress' property, and I must do my mistress' bidding, whether it's a spoken command or a physical force. I am happy to say that I am a slave! And I am proud to be one!"

The other slaves on the floor broke into spontaneous applause. After a moment, they stopped and looked at Wendy, remembering their place. But Wendy smiled and nodded, and the applause continued—with the exception of Margot, who looked sullenly at the woman who had just found her calling.

"I think you should welcome Leslie into the fold," Wendy said, and as Wendy took her place, the others hugged and kissed her, congratulating her on her discovery. Then Leslie turned to her teacher, smiling. "Thank you, Mistress Wendy, thank you!" she cried. "I am forever in your debt, Mistress Wendy!"

"That will be enough," Wendy said, returning instantly to her role as teacher. The classroom instantly became quiet, all eyes on her. Their moment of gaiety, allowed by their teacher, was over. They were once again slaves.

"We will get on with our lesson," Wendy said, picking up her riding crop and using it to point at Brenda. "Up here, right now. And Margot, you come here as well."

Once again Margot was ordered to put a restraint on her fellow slave; this time, it was a cruel leather cone that was slipped over Brenda's head. It was big enough that it completely covered her torso, with only her head sticking out through the hole in the top. A strap was passed between her legs and buckled so that she was unable to move her arms at all. A second strap was tightened around the cone to hold her firmly.

"In this device," Wendy said, "your mistress can control you completely." She used her stiletto-heeled boot to push the kneeling slave over. Brenda could do nothing but fall on her side, unable to put out her hands to break her fall. Margot sucked in her breath quickly as she saw how helpless Brenda was. Why couldn't she be the one in the leather cone!

Wendy demonstrated a few more features of the cone, and showed how a mistress might open the straps to allow a bit of a movement, or tighten them completely so that a slave would not even be able to wiggle her fingers. Then, on Wendy's orders, Margot slowly unbuckled the straps and pulled the cone roughly over Brenda's head. Both of them returned to their places and knelt on the floor.

Wendy decided it was time for Margot to receive a little extra training. Since mild punishment was the reward that Margot so badly craved, Wendy thought that she would prove to the gorgeous slave that here no rewards were given out unless orders were obeyed, and obeyed immediately without question or hesitation. Since she was still hot and wet from riding Leslie around the room, Wendy thought that she might combine a little lesson with a bit of pleasure. She opened the metal snaps that held the crotch of her leather catsuit closed and pulled the flaps back. Her beautiful dark pussy was exposed, shiny with juice and throbbing with excitement.

She walked over to Margot, who knelt on the floor before her, and stood so that her pussy was right over the slave. "Pleasure me," she ordered.

Margot looked at her for a moment, then turned her head and said, "You're not my mistress."

The room was deathly silent, and then a loud collective gasp went up from the other four slaves. None of them could believe it. Their shock immediately turned to dread as they looked at Wendy's face.

Margot, too, was silent as she met Wendy's eyes. Her words, so carelessly thrown out, had doomed her and she knew it. Instantly she was on the floor, crying out, "Mistress, I'm sorry! Please forgive me, Mistress! I didn't know what I was saying! Please, Mistress, mercy!"

Wendy's controlled fury made her voice so cold that Alicia closed her eyes and tried to shrink away. "Too late for that, you stupid, worthless fuck," Wendy told Margot, who was on her belly on the floor. "I don't really think you understand just what kind of a predicament your mouth has gotten you into. I don't want to hear another word out of you until I order you to speak. By that time you will be grateful to obey every command any mistress ever gives you."

She reached down and wrapped her fist around Margot's heavy collar, then dragged her on the floor over to the wall. Although she struggled, Margot was no match for the powerful mistress and she could only sob as her spine bumped on the hard floor.

At the wall, Wendy selected the gruesome

leather mask. Roughly she pulled it down over Margot's face and snapped it closed around her neck. Then once again she pulled the tall slave over the floor to the front of the class. Margot's sobs were muffled by the black leather as Wendy swiftly handcuffed her wrists together behind her back.

"I will never give a command that will not be obeyed!" Wendy hissed. The other four slaves cringed, but Wendy ignored them completely. This was the turning point and they all knew it. Wendy would not stop this lesson now until Margot was completely, entirely broken.

"Stick your tongue out!" Wendy ordered, but Margot was sobbing too hard to obey. Ruthlessly Wendy picked up the riding crop and stuck the handle inside Margot's mouth. She pushed down on her tongue and forced her to stick it out. Then she pulled the zipper across. Margot's tongue stuck out of the side of the leather mouth. She couldn't pull it back in because the edges of the zipper bit into the tender side of her tongue; she had to leave it right where it was, stuck grotesquely out of the corner of the leather opening.

"I gave you an order, and you are going to carry it out!" Wendy said. She dragged Margot upright on her knees by the heavy leather collar. Then, with a hand on either side of the leather-clad head, Wendy pulled Margot against her pussy. Margot's tongue, pulled out and held tight by the mask's zipper, rubbed against her clit.

While the rest of the class watched, horrified and yet fascinated, Wendy used Margot's tongue like a dildo. Margot gasped and cried but was helpless as her tongue was rubbed against Wendy's hot, wet clit.

Wendy pleasured herself with the slave's tongue. To her delight she found it exciting. The domineering slave was now totally under her control! The thought made her pussy burn even more, and she cooled it with the tip of Margot's tongue. She pressed back and forth, pushing against her clit, ignoring Margot's sobs and concentrating on how good her pussy felt to have the unwilling tongue rubbed against it.

Her clit was throbbing with a life of its own. "Suck my pussy, scum!" she whispered, and roughly maneuvered Margot's head. Spreading her legs wide apart, she moved forward until Margot's tongue was on the entrance to her tunnel, then she pushed back so that the tip was pressing her clit. Hot rushes went through her body, born both of sex and dominance. It was the ultimate reward for a mistress—to humiliate completely, to dominate absolutely! It was Wendy's finest hour and she gloried in it.

"Never again will you deny a mistress!" she told Margot, as she pushed and pulled at the masked woman. "Never again will you disobey a command!"

She rubbed hard against her clit. The mask was now soaked with her pussy juice. Margot, in agony, was unable to do anything but submit to her mistress' whims. At one point she fell back on her heels, but Wendy grabbed her by the heavy collar and roughly pulled her back upright so that her tongue would once again reach Wendy's wet cunt.

She pushed Margot away for a moment and cried, "Will you disobey me again?" Unable to answer, Margot shook her head no. Immediately her swollen tongue, cramped in its position and cut by the cruel metal zipper, was pushed back against Wendy's clit. After a moment, she was pushed back again. "Will you obey your commands when they're given?" The leather mask nodded assent, and was again forced back to Wendy's cunt. "Have you learned your lesson?" More nodding, and again the rough push back to the swollen clit.

Wendy was now using Margot's tongue not to punish her, but to please herself. The most delicious sensations were running through her whole body as she rubbed her clit on Margot's tongue. A heady rush went though her and she trembled just a bit. Then her clit exploded and she ground Margot's head against her cunt as she went over the edge and came.

Once the last swell had died down, there was no basking in the afterglow. Immediately she grabbed Margot's collar and dragged her across the floor. The leather mask was shiny with a mixture of saliva, pussy juice and a bit of thin, watery blood from the cut on Margot's tongue. Still unable to pull her tongue back in because of the zipper's teeth, Margot was limp, her tongue sticking out foolishly from the side of the mouth. There was no fight left in her at all.

She was dragged to her feet before she even realized what was going on; then, roughly, Wendy shoved her into the leather sling that hung from the ceiling. Face down in the sling, Margot could only whimper and lie still. Her hands were still cuffed behind her back and she was completely at Wendy's mercy.

Wendy was anything but merciful. "There's something to be said for you, worm," Wendy said scornfully. "At least I'm getting a chance to try out all my new purchases." She went through the large bag and then walked back to the sling where Margot was held.

The first item was a pair of nipple clamps, but these were especially nasty ones. Attached to each clamp was a small, thin chain, and at the end of the chain was a small lead weight. Reaching under the sling, Wendy pulled Margot's nipples between the straps of the sling. Margot cried out as a clamp was snapped onto each nipple. The weights pulled them down, and the other four slaves winced as they saw Margot's breasts stretched out, the nipples held by the metal clasps.

The second object was even worse. It was a large purple dildo, long and thick, with a huge knobby head. Without any ceremony, Wendy spread Margot's asscheeks and jammed the dildo inside. Margot screamed, muffled by the leather mask.

Then, calmly, Wendy looked over her handiwork, smiled, and returned to the front of the class. The four slaves were as attentive as they could possibly be when, to their shock, Wendy casually went right back to the lesson she had been giving before Margot had given her such trouble. When ordered, Ellen stood at the front of the class, and Wendy demonstrated the proper way to stand when a slave was required to wear a leather device that chained her ankles to a collar around her throat.

All of them ignored the slave in the corner, Wendy because it was part of her plan, and the other students because they dared not turn around and look. It was difficult for them not to. Margot was anything but quiet about her agony. Occasionally she would sob hysterically, and then calm down to a whimper. Once she tried to squirm in the sling, but screamed when the nipple weights and the dildo in her ass moved. Wendy smiled to herself. Everyone has a breaking point, she thought. I finally found this one's.

The lesson went on for half an hour, then Wendy walked to the back of the room where Margot hung helpless. Because the leather mask covered her ears, Margot wasn't aware that Wendy was beside her. Wendy reached under the sling, grabbed the nipple weights, and yanked them off by their chains. Margot almost blacked out, and her muffled scream was so loud that the other slaves were chilled through. Alicia's hands went to her own nipples in sympathy. Wendy laughed. "I knew they must hurt as much coming off as they do on," she told the helpless slave. "Enjoy it while you can, scum." Then she walked back to the front of the room and continued with a new lesson on proper grooming.

Two more hours passed before the evening's class was finally over. Wendy had the four slaves turn around to face the sling. It was a good lesson for them as well, she said to herself. She didn't expect to have any trouble from any of them again.

First, she roughly pulled the dildo out of Margot's ass. Margot was too exhausted to do anything but whimper. "You're lucky I'm feeling very nice tonight," Wendy told her. "Any other time I would have ordered you to clean it off with your tongue."

The handcuffs came off next. Margot's arms were so swollen and stiff she could not move them. Roughly Wendy pushed them down beside her body and, again, Margot could only whimper. When she was shoved out of the sling, her knees gave out and she feel to the floor. Wendy left her there and pulled off the mask.

Margot didn't even look human. Her hair was plastered to her head with sweat and her skin was a horrible mottled red. Her eyes were swollen and red-rimmed from crying. Her face was smeared with tears and mucous and there was blood on her chin from the cut on her tongue. Her lips were swollen and she moved her jaw painfully.

"I hope we've learned something here tonight," Wendy said.

"Yes, Mistress." It was a whisper through painful lips.

"Go clean yourself up," Wendy ordered. "You make me sick looking at you." She held out the horrible leather mask. "Clean this up as well, and hurry back."

"Yes, Mistress," Margot said, and immediately struggled to her feet and took the mask. Walking stiffly, she hurried out the door. They could hear water running down the hall and shortly afterward, Margot hurried back. Her face was washed but still mottled red, her lips and tongue swollen. Immediately she dropped to her knees before Wendy, put her head down, and offered the cleaned leather mask.

"Thank you, slave," Wendy said, taking it and hanging it back up on its peg on the wall.

"May I have permission to speak, Mistress?" Margot asked.

Wendy thrilled to hear her. "Yes, slave," she said.

"Mistress, I'm sorry." It was difficult for her to form the words with her tongue so badly swollen. "I'm sorry I acted the way I did. I have learned my lesson. I am a slave. You are my Mistress. I will not forget that."

Wendy didn't think she'd ever heard sweeter words. "Don't ever forget, slave," she said. "Now, class, you are dismissed."

She watched as they chimed, "Thank you, Mistress," then stood up to leave. It had been a very important night for all of them. Brenda, Alicia, and Ellen had learned an essential lesson about how ruthless their teacher could be if provoked. Leslie had discovered her true identity. And Margot, who had been such a worthless waste of time, had started to blossom into the truly magnificent slave that both

Leah and Wendy had known she had the potential to become. Once again Wendy felt the leather catsuit grow warm and wet between her legs.

"All but you," Wendy indicated to Brenda as the slaves passed out the door in front of her.

"Thank you, Mistress," Brenda replied gratefully, and immediately knelt on the floor, ready for a command. With all her heart, she hoped that the spot before her mistress' door would be hers again this night.

Wendy watched as the slaves dressed, carefully fastening the top buttons of their shirts so that the leather collars would not be visible. She then stood at the top of the stairs as they filed out of the house into the cool, black night.

She turned and walked back to the classroom, taking off the skin-hugging catsuit as she went. Her nipples were hard and she tweaked them with her fingers, then went inside. Brenda, she knew, would be only too eager to take care of the rest.

NINE

As silent as a whisper, the Cadillac limousine turned the corner. Comfortable in the luxurious back seat, Wendy took a sip of the champagne she held, and looked through the darkened windows. The city streets were ablaze with lights and crowded with people rushing off to their evening engagements. Wendy just smiled to herself and sipped again.

She stretched out her legs, clad in black fishnet stockings. Her shoes were impossibly high and the buckles were finished off with tiny silver padlocks. Her suit was made of the same rich, shiny black leather, a sexy one-piece affair that dipped low between her breasts and gave onlookers just a teasing glance at their magnificence. Cut high in the crotch and as tight as a second skin, it showed off her beautiful body to its fullest advantage. It was the first time she had worn it; nothing but a new suit would do for this most special occasion.

She had told the class to think of it as a "school field trip," but, of course, it was much more than that. It was a special one-night event for mistresses and their slaves at a lavish hotel and she was going to use it both as a special lesson and as a coming-out party for her students.

She was finally confident enough in them to make the arrangements. All of them were doing exceptionally in her class, especially Margot. The night spent in the sling had been the turning point. Now it seemed that she couldn't do enough for her teacher, and, at times, the other slaves were jealous of how well she performed.

Just as the limousine pulled up at the front of the hotel, Wendy noticed that her five students were getting out of a taxi parked a respectable distance from the front door. As they noticed the Cadillac, they hurried and waited by the side of the building. It wouldn't have done for them to make a grand entrance in the hotel's driveway, but they also didn't want to be a second late for their mistress' arrival. Wendy looked at her watch and smiled. They were precisely on time.

The car pulled up in front of the hotel, and the driver got out and opened the back door for her. Her costume was covered by a long coat, but the driver was still intrigued by the stiletto-heeled shoes with their silver ornaments. Wendy, of course, ignored him, except to tell him that he was to wait for her no matter how long she was. Likewise, she ignored the doorman who held the door while the regal mistress and her five students walked inside.

At the entrance to the ballroom, Wendy gave them permission to remove their coats. She checked them over. They all had matching outfits, made of red leather straps and chrome rings, which concealed their pussies but fitted around their exposed breasts so that they stood out beautifully. Their everyday leather collars had been replaced by matching red ones, accented with chrome studs and rings for leashes.

Wendy checked her own coat, then ordered them into the position she had taught them earlier. She had arrived late to make an entrance and was determined to do so. Her own slave, Brenda, was behind her. Margot was at the end of the line. Nodding to the woman at the door, Wendy walked into the party.

Everyone nearby stopped and stared as the class and their teacher entered. Wendy never looked better, and the five slaves in their matching outfits made a magnificent entourage. As she had expected, Wendy heard the crowd gasp as the final slaves walked into the room. Margot was gorgeous enough to be on the cover of every fashion magazine in the country. Instead, she was here, clad in a leather suit that showed off her perfect breasts, walking behind a mistress whose every desire was her command.

Through the grapevine, almost every mistress at the party had heard about Wendy and her school, and they flocked to talk to her. The slaves stood as they had been taught while Wendy shook hands, and hugged and kissed and greeted the women who came forward.

When everyone nearby had been greeted, Wendy turned to Brenda. "Drink," she said abruptly, and Brenda rushed to get one for her mistress. She presented it, kneeling, then immediately went back to her place behind her beloved mistress. It was a very special night for her as well. Of the entire class, she was the one chosen to serve her mistress, the one who walked directly behind her. She couldn't have been happier.

"Wendy! Good to see you!" Wendy turned to greet a friend who was looking over the five slaves carefully.

"Susan! I haven't seen you for so long," Wendy said, kissing her. The woman was tall and blonde, clad in a leather bra and garter; the small slave who stood behind her wore nothing but a collar. The leash attached to it was in Susan's hand. The little slave's eyes were glued to her mistress and the devotion in them was beautiful to see.

"So this is your class, is it?" Susan said. "Wendy, it looks like you've been really busy with them. And this one—this isn't the one that Leah was telling me about, is it?"

"Certainly is," Wendy said, indicating the beautiful slave who kept her eyes deferentially on the floor. "Margot, come here." Margot obeyed immediately.

"Oh, it can't be," Susan laughed. "The one Leah told me about wouldn't have obeyed you like that."

"Oh, it is," Wendy said. "This slave and I came to a little understanding not long ago. She was just as bad as Leah described. You'll notice there's been a bit of a change. Slave, tell Mistress Susan what happened."

"Mistress Wendy taught me about being a slave, Mistress," Margot said. "I owe it to her."

Susan looked the tall slave over. "I am so jealous of Leah!" she said. "She really is as beautiful as Leah said she was. Wendy, she's a credit to your school. That reminds me," she added, taking a sip of her drink, "Will you be holding more classes once this one graduates?"

"Definitely," Wendy said. "It's too much fun to quit now!"

"Then I'm getting my order in right now," Susan said. "I have another one at home. I couldn't bring her here tonight—too rough. She really tries hard, but she doesn't quite come up to my standards. I want to put her into your next class.

"I couldn't help overhearing!" another mistress said, leading over a pair of slaves who were handcuffed together and held by a leash. "Are you taking on more students, Wendy? Save me two spots. After seeing what you've done with those five, I won't let you leave here until you agree to sign me up in the next class!"

The requests turned into a deluge. Suddenly everyone was around Wendy, examining the slaves that stood so quietly behind her, demanding a spot in her classroom. Wendy could hardly believe it, and she congratulated herself on bringing the students to the party. Within half an hour, she had her next class filled and was taking names for the class following that one. Never had she dreamed that there would be such a demand for her services.

Her slaves, as well, were having a special night of their own. While they were all very careful to keep their pride well hidden, Wendy didn't miss a few of their glances at other slaves, or the looks that her charges got from other women in chains and collars. It was obvious to other slaves that these were different, having been honed to their maximum potential. Their rigorous training was evident in the way they carried themselves and the way they served Wendy instantly whenever she ordered them to do anything. While the other slaves were attentive to their mistresses and obeyed them completely, it was easy to see that a few of them were jealous that they had not been schooled in their tasks as these privileged five had been.

Wendy made her way through the party, greeting

old friends and making introductions with new ones. The entire time, her class's behavior was beyond reproach. A few times Wendy glanced back, just to make sure that the tall slave at the end of the line was in form. She needn't have worried. Margot was indeed the perfect submissive that Leah had known all along she could become. Wendy smiled. When they got back to class, she just might snap on some nipple clamps as a reward. Margot still craved pain and Wendy now used it as an incentive rather than a punishment.

"Wendy!" She turned and saw a tall, beautiful Japanese woman walking toward her. She was dressed in a skin-tight miniskirt and a short motorcycle jacket, hung with chrome rings and bright chains, with nothing under it. A tantalizing glimpse of her breasts was visible, and Wendy noticed a tiny tattoo on the side of one.

"Elizabeth! Good to see you," Wendy said, and even though she didn't know the lovely woman all that well, Elizabeth brushed her cheek with a kiss before stepping forward to glimpse Wendy's leather-clad students.

"So these are the ones, are they?" Elizabeth looked them over carefully. She put one well-manicured hand under Ellen's chin to lift it, and Ellen kept her eyes down properly. "It looks like you've done a good job, Wendy."

"I think I have," Wendy said proudly. "The school worked out even better than I expected."

Elizabeth went down the line of slaves, who kept very still, their eyes on the ground. When she came to Margot, she let out a low whistle. "My heavens, they weren't kidding, were they?" she said. "Wendy, she's magnificent."

"She is now," Wendy said, and she noticed just

the lightest flush on Margot's cheeks. "It took a lot of work, but I think it was worth it."

"I heard all about that, too," Elizabeth said. "Your reputation's perfect just on this one alone." Addressed Margot directly, she said, "You're a very lucky slut. Most mistresses would have just thrown you out. You owe Mistress Wendy a great deal."

"Yes, Mistress," Margot replied, bowing her head just the proper degree. "I'm very grateful to my teacher, Mistress."

Elizabeth walked back up the line. "Well, it should be fun to do this group, Wendy," she said. "Everything that you ordered is finished. Whenever you're ready to have it done, you just give me a call."

"It will be very soon now," Wendy promised. "Their final examinations are this week, and then we'll be ready for graduation."

She and Elizabeth accepted fresh drinks from a slave carrying a tray through the party, and walked over to greet another group of friends. Still in their perfect row, their eyes afire with devotion for their teacher, her slaves followed every step she took.

Alicia looked at the cork carefully, and then inserted the tip of the corkscrew into it. She prayed that it wouldn't crumble and deposit even a single shred of cork into the wine below. As she slid it out of the bottle, she held her breath. A light film of sweat was on her upper lip, and she breathed a quiet sigh of relief when the cork slid out whole.

After wrapping a clean white cloth around the neck of the bottle, she poured a small splash into the glass, and presented it to Wendy. Once her teacher had sampled the wine, she filled the glass to its proper level and once again presented it in the manner she hoped would be most pleasing to her mistress.

Wendy took the wine, sipped it, and then set it down beside her on the table. "You may sit down," she said, and then wrote on the piece of paper attached to her clipboard. Alicia had no way of knowing what was written, but once again she prayed, this time for favorable marks on this, her final exam.

One by one, the students went up to the table and showed their expertise in opening and serving wine. Each time, Wendy offered no comments on their performance, but simply wrote on her clipboard, and by the end of the exercise, all looked exhausted with worry. The notes would decide whether they would pass or fail!

The tests were done randomly to catch them off guard. Sometimes all five would be ordered to perform the same task; sometimes just one or two. They did not know what order the tasks would come in, or even if the subjects they had painstakingly studied would be tested. The only thing they knew for certain was that they had to perform everything flawlessly.

They quickly learned that anything could happen. In the middle of pouring coffee, Leslie was ordered to lick her mistress' shoes. Wendy was glad to notice that there was not even a moment's hesitation when the command was given. Leslie immediately put down the coffeepot and rushed to fall on her belly and apply her tongue to Wendy's shiny patent-leather shoes. When Wendy indicated that the job was done, Leslie begged permission to empty the half-filled cup so as to pour her mistress a fresh, hot one. Wendy nodded, and made a notation on her clipboard.

Every aspect of their submission was tested, as they discovered one day when Wendy walked into the class wearing only stockings, garter, and gloves. She stood before Margot. "Pleasure me," she ordered.

Not too long before, that order had set off a disastrous chain of events for the tall, gorgeous slave. This time there was nothing but complete submission. Murmuring, "Yes, Mistress! Thank you, Mistress," the slave applied her tongue to her teacher's delicious dark pussy.

How delicious it was indeed! Margot was pleased to find Wendy's cunt was already wet, and she eagerly lapped up the juice with her tongue. She had learned an amazingly wide range of techniques in this school and she put several of them to use.

First her tongue circled Wendy's lips, teasing just to the point that Wendy would allow. Then she pushed her tongue out fully and slid it between the tips, pushing against the point of Wendy's clit. Wendy was careful not to let her expression give her away, but inside, she was reveling in the sweet, icy-hot chills that ran from her clit right out to her fingers and toes.

Margot's face was soon wet with Wendy's juice. She licked at the entrance to Wendy's hole and pushed her tongue in as far as she possibly could. As the other students watched, jealous that it was Margot and not them pleasing the teacher, she moved back and forth between the sensitive points of Wendy's pussy. Her tongue flashed quickly over the clit; she took a few slow, full laps, and then went back to the rapid thrusts that she knew her teacher so enjoyed.

The room was silent but for the lapping and sucking. The students, having been given permission to watch, saw Margot arch her back and press her mouth against Wendy's pussy to take the clit between her lips and tickle it with the tip of her tongue.

Without warning, Wendy stepped back, then moved over to Leslie. "Finish the job," she ordered, and watched Margot out of the corner of her eye. Margot's expression did not change even though she was disappointed that she had to stop. A mistress had decided that another slave should take over and because Margot was only a slave herself, she had to accept that without question. She noticed that even in her disappointment, she was thrilled. She had to do exactly what her mistress ordered because she was nothing but a slave!

Leslie took over eagerly, after thanking her mistress for the opportunity. Like Margot she had a wide repertoire of styles, and she started by working her tongue in a circle around Wendy's clit before pressing it back and forth with her lips. Also like Margot she happily lapped up the thick, creamy nectar from her teacher's pussy and longed for more.

The other slaves watched as Leslie pushed her tongue against Wendy's clit and shook her head back and forth to flash over it. Wendy was on fire with the heat from her pussy and the slave's tongue felt so good! The novice had blossomed so beautifully. Wendy closed her eyes for a moment as Leslie's tongue worked like a finger on her cunt. Anne would be so pleased with her slave, now trained to perfection!

Leslie licked and sucked, both from obedience and from love of licking her mistress. Wendy felt her belly tighten. Then within seconds, all in a rush, the orgasm overcame her. She was so strong that no one in the room realized what had happened. But as she stepped back from Leslie without a word, her skin was so sensitive it felt as if it was on fire, and her pussy throbbed and quivered with a mind of its own. It was the ultimate glory of being a mistress, of giving commands that filled her with such delicious feelings.

The examinations went on for a week, until the five slaves were a mass of nerves, fearful that one tiny slip might ruin their chances for graduation. Each movement of Wendy's pen on the clipboard kept them wondering. A smile from her was enough to raise their spirits for the day; the slightest frown could make them worry all night, tossing and turning because they were too upset to sleep.

They needn't have worried. At the end of the week, Wendy stood before the five naked slaves, all of them still in their heavy leather classroom collars.

"Your week of examinations has gone quite well," she informed them. "I believe I have taken you through almost every type of service you will ever be required to perform for a mistress. Many people don't realized it, but the things they consider to be trivial are often the most important, and they are the things that you must always strive to complete with perfection. A slave who can impart pleasure with her tongue is absolutely worthless if she can't properly serve a glass of wine.

"That is why we spent so much time on what may have seemed to you to be minor items, and why you were so well tested in them. Any slave can lick a mistress' boots or kneel before her for punishment. You are beyond that. You can serve your mistresses, accompany them, serve their guests, all because you have received training that ordinary slaves have not."

She allowed herself the faintest smile at them. "I am pleased to inform you," she said, "that all of you have passed with honors."

There was a collective sigh, many smiles, and a chorus of, "Thank you, Mistress! Oh, thank you!" If they had been given permission they would have danced around the room. But Wendy was pleased to see that no matter how excited they were, all of them kept to their positions and did nothing more than they were allowed.

"In four days, there will be a graduation ceremony," Wendy continued. "At that point you will receive your honors. I will not tell you what they will be except to inform you that undoubtedly your mistresses will command you to wear them at all times. They will mark you as graduates of my school, as slaves who were trained as such for the sole purpose of serving their mistresses."

She walked back to the head of the classroom. "You will not wear them with pride, of course, because you are nothing but slaves and you are not permitted to be proud," she continued. "You will wear them as a reminder of what you are, lowly slaves whose only mission in life is obeying commands, no matter which mistress gives them to you."

She looked at them, all kneeling on the hard wooden floor, all of them with their eyes on the floor, all of them thrilled as could be with their accomplishment. "Now go," she said. "In four days I will see you all again, and you will never be quite the same."

TEN

Leah knocked at the door of Wendy's house. In seconds, it was opened by Brenda, who as Wendy's personal slave had been given the privilege of serving guests before and after the graduation ceremonies. Brenda led her to the living room, politely asked if she may serve a drink, and then hurried off to prepare a glass while Leah joined the others.

The mistresses were all present, having sent their slaves over earlier to prepare for the ceremonies. Dressed in their very best, holding glasses of fine champagne between well-manicured fingers, Diane, Anne, and Wendy each kissed Leah and congratulated her on her slave's graduation with honors.

"Where are they, Wendy?" Leah asked. "I only saw your own wench."

"They're getting ready for the ceremony," Wendy explained. "I put them in the spare rooms for now. At the moment it's best. I don't want them getting too excited."

The mistresses chatted among themselves, and Leah took the glass of champagne offered by Brenda. She lifted it in a toast. "To Wendy!" she said. "To the teacher who took our rough, unpolished sluts and turned them into slaves we can be proud to own."

"To Wendy!" the others repeated, and Wendy beamed as the three mistresses sipped their champagne. She was so proud of her school and of the job she had done on the five slaves.

There was a knock at the door and Brenda rushed to open it. Waiting on the step was the beautiful, tall Japanese woman from the party.

"Come in, please, Mistress," Brenda said, and closed the door behind the woman before taking her thin jacket. She also offered to take Elizabeth's bag, but the woman kept it with her.

"Your mistress is expecting me," Elizabeth said, and followed Brenda to the living room. As soon as she saw her guest, Wendy rushed over to greet her. Brenda, meanwhile, disappeared into the kitchen for another drink.

"Elizabeth! So glad to see you," Wendy said, kissing her cheek. "Ladies, I would like you to meet Elizabeth." she made the introductions. "Elizabeth will be a very important part of our ceremony today," she said mysteriously. "I'm sure you will very much appreciate her handiwork."

"Pleased to meet you all," Elizabeth said, and shook hands with the three women before accepting a glass of champagne from Brenda. "I saw your slaves at the party Wendy attended. I'm sure you're all very happy with the job Wendy has done."

Wendy motioned for Brenda to come to her; the blonde slave did so immediately. "Yes, Mistress?"

"Inform the other slaves that we will be calling for them in about an hour," Wendy said. "They should be ready the moment we require them."

"Yes, Mistress," she said, and hurried away down the hall.

The slaves had been sequestered into two spare bedrooms, in pairs so that they could help each other to get ready. Brenda opened the first door, and gave the message to Leslie and Margot, then informed Alicia and Ellen, who were waiting in the second bedroom, sitting on the large bed.

The door closed again behind Brenda, and Alicia looked over at Ellen. Their heavy, everyday classroom collars were gone and both were completely naked. On the dresser sat their combs and brushes, along with the beautiful new velvet collars they would wear for the ceremony. There were also two mortarboards for them to put on their heads in recognition of their graduation.

"Another hour," Alicia lamented. "I can hardly wait! Why do we have to sit here another hour?"

"Hush your mouth!" Ellen said sharply. "Mistress Wendy has ordered us to wait for an hour and we will do it! I would wait ten hours if Mistress Wendy ordered me," she added.

"Well, I would wait ten hours, too," Alicia said. "It's just that I'm so excited about the ceremony, I'm hardly able to sit still. I'm so horny you couldn't possibly imagine it. My poor pussy is just begging for some attention." Slowly, gently, she reached over and stroked Ellen's arm.

"Stop that!" Ellen jerked her arm away as if it had been burned. "We're not allowed to do that! We're slaves!"

"I know that," Alicia said slowly, leaning across

the bed to touch Ellen again. "But I'm such a horny slave. And who would ever know?"

"Mistress Wendy might find out!" Ellen warned.

"How?" Alicia asked. "You heard Brenda. They won't be back for us for another hour. There's a lot you can do in an hour, when no one's going to disturb you."

"Well, it's just not right," Ellen said.

"I know it's not right," Alicia agreed. "But my poor pussy doesn't seem to realize it. Aren't you horny too?"

"Well, yes," Ellen reluctantly admitted. "But I can't do something like that. Mistress Wendy wouldn't allow it."

Alicia put her hand on Ellen's leg and noticed, to her joy, that while Ellen trembled slightly she did not pull away. Encouraged, she caressed Ellen's skin. This time there was no resistance at all, and Alicia knew that she was winning.

"Mistress Wendy will never know," Alicia whispered, and drew herself up so that she was kneeling behind Ellen. Her hot breath tickled the back of Ellen's neck when she pulled the hair away, and she kissed softly, working her way around to Ellen's face.

"It's not right," Ellen said, but her words were stopped by Alicia's kiss. Her pussy was throbbing too much and she could not resist any longer. She met Alicia's mouth, hungry as a starving woman, and they breathed deeply and searched each other's mouths with their probing tongues. Finally meeting the touch she so desperately craved, Alicia's hands moved all over her sister slave.

Both knew it was wrong, but the love-famished slaves had gone too far to stop. They were careful to keep their moans quiet, but Ellen couldn't suppress a gasp when she felt Alicia's hands on her breasts. Then, suddenly, Alicia's tongue was on her nipples.

She turned around on the bed so that they could suck on each other's tits at the same time.

"They're so good," Alicia whispered, and sucked Ellen's nipple in between her lips. Ellen groaned softly and ran her tongue all around Alicia's breast before flicking back and forth over the nipple, which became rock-hard. Alicia's hand moved down slowly and found its spot between Ellen's legs. It was no surprise to her when her fingers came away soaking wet.

"You want this as badly as I do," she said, probing the depths of Ellen's pussy with her fingers.

Ellen did. "I want to taste your pussy!" she whispered. "Please let me lick it. Please lick mine!"

"Move down, then," the young, black-haired slave said. They positioned themselves so that they could suck each other's pussies.

It was the hottest sixty-nine Alicia could remember. She had to bite her tongue to keep from crying out when Ellen's tongue touched her swollen, needful clit. Ellen's clit was just as wanting, and Alicia lost no time in putting her mouth to it and sucking.

They lashed over each other's pussies like crazy women. Each was grinding her cunt into the other's tongue in a hot sexual frenzy, gasping at the sensations that flowed through them as they did.

"Harder!" Alicia gasped, and Ellen pushed her tongue against her partner's clit as firmly as she could. There was no grace, no teasing, just raw movements from women who had been denied them for so long. All of their careful training was forgotten in their quest to simply come. Alicia's mouth was glued to Ellen's clit, and she sucked it as hard as she could. Ellen lapped Alicia's clit with an intensity that surprised her.

Soaked with sweat, the two slaves writhed on the bed, Alicia on top, Ellen below, their fingers pushed into wet, velvety cunts. "Fuck me with your hand!" Alicia begged, and Ellen pushed and pulled at Alicia's hole while her tongue never stopped its relentless flicking on her clit.

They were so close to coming! Their pussies were tight, throbbing, filling their whole bodies with hot waves. Only a few more seconds, Ellen thought, and my cunt will explode! How good that would feel....

They were so involved that they never heard the footsteps in the hall, never noticed the door handle turning, never even realized that Wendy was in the room until they heard her shriek, *"What the fuck do you think you're doing?"*

Their blood went cold with the shock. Their sexual appetite was completely forgotten as they glimpsed their teacher, her face filled with rage, standing in the doorway. Instantly Ellen was on the floor, groveling before her mistress.

"Please, Mistress Wendy!" she pleaded. "I didn't want to do it!" Tears began to stream from her eyes and she sobbed. "I didn't want to, she forced me! Please Mistress Wendy, please believe me!"

A savage kick shut her up and sent her sprawling to the floor. "Not another word out of either of you!" Wendy hissed.

Alicia was still on the bed. Wendy grabbed a fistful of her long black hair and pulled her onto the floor. Alicia screamed in fear and pain. With her other hand, Wendy grabbed Ellen by the hair. She dragged them from the room, and they struggled to keep on their feet, sobbing. When they fell, Wendy's strong arms dragged them up again by their hair.

They found themselves being dragged into the classroom, which had been festively decorated for the graduation ceremonies. The three mistresses and Elizabeth were relaxing in comfortable chairs in the room, but all rose to their feet when Wendy dragged the two into the room and threw them harshly on the hard floor.

"Wendy! What's wrong?" Diane asked.

"These two," Wendy said, indicating the slaves sobbing at her feet, "were in their room having sex together!"

The mistresses gasped with shock; then, instantly, Diane and Leah looked as furious as Wendy had as they glared at their slaves.

Still trying to escape punishment, Ellen threw herself on the floor before Leah. "Please, Mistress!" she sobbed. "Alicia forced me to do it! Mistress Wendy didn't realize! I didn't—" but she was silenced again, this time by a fierce backhanded blow that knocked her against the wall. Dazed, she stayed on the floor, sobbing, too frightening to look into her mistress' face.

"I might have expected this from Margot," Leah said. "But not from you, Ellen! I thought you would be so good! And now you have shamed me and shamed yourself. This will not be forgotten."

"No, Mistress," Ellen moaned, and tried to blend into the wall. It struck her that her best plan at that moment would simply be to remain silent, and she did.

Alicia, meanwhile, was cowering under Diane's infuriated glare. "I had such hopes for you," Diane said, slowly and coldly. "We will discuss this further when we get home." Alicia curled into a ball and trembled, trying, like Ellen, to just disappear.

"I'm very sorry," Wendy told Leah and Diane, "but you understand that I can't let these two graduate after such an episode."

"I understand, Wendy," Diane said, and Leah nodded. "There's really nothing you could have done to prevent it. Who would have thought they would have done such a thing?"

"Well, they will receive further lessons, and I will test them again," Wendy continued. "There are no failures in this school. They will graduate, and they will earn their honors; it will just take a little more time. Of course, there will be no charge for the necessary extra schooling."

She looked at the two cowering on the floor, their faces bloodlessly white, and she thought of something. "They have shamed themselves tonight," she said. "With your permission, I would like them to receive their first lesson. I would like to teach them what it's like for someone else to really shame them."

"Go ahead, Wendy," Diane said.

Leah added, "She's all yours. Do your worst."

Wendy left the room, and came back a little while later. She stood at the front of the classroom, while Elizabeth and the three mistresses returned to their chairs.

"As you know," she began, "a very embarrassing incident took place here this evening." She indicated the two disgraced slaves, who wisely had not moved from their spots against the wall.

"These two thought they might enjoy a little bit of sex. They knew it was wrong of them to do so, but they went ahead and carried out their plan anyway. It was a very bad judgement call. They will not graduate tonight and will be held back for extra lessons. That first lesson will take place tonight, right here, in front of all of us."

Alicia and Ellen looked at each other, their faces masks of fear. There was also fury in Ellen's eyes, for the slave that had persuaded her into the situation in the first place.

"When I was a child," Wendy continued, "it was

very common to take a disobedient child and give her exactly what it was she craved. If a child thought she might like to smoke, the parents would often give her a big cigar and stand by while they made her smoke the whole thing. It was usually enough to persuade her that perhaps she really didn't want whatever it was she thought she desired."

She turned to the two slaves, who shrank back from her stare. "You two wanted sex," she said. "And so you shall have it."

She went to the doorway and indicated that the slaves standing in the hallway should come in. They did. Brenda, Leslie, and Margot entered the room, and the eyes of the shamed slaves widened with horror. All three of them were wearing huge dildos strapped to them.

"Both of you sank low enough to turn to another slave for your sexual pleasures," Wendy said. "For a mistress to command pleasure from a slave is one thing. But to beg your pleasure from another submissive as you have done—well, I'm only glad that I shall never have to do such a disgraceful thing."

She walked over to Alicia and once again grabbed her by a fistful of her long black hair. Dragging her to the front of the room, she forced the young slave to her hands and knees so that her ass was up in the air. She then motioned for Leslie to come over.

"Now," Wendy said, coldly, "you will beg for this slave's dick in your cunt."

Alicia hesitated, puzzled by the strange command. Her instant reward was a slice from the riding crop that Wendy grabbed. The welt rose on her skin and was joined by a second. The lesson was clear.

"Please," Alicia said woodenly to the slave who stood before her, "put your dick in my cunt."

Furious, Wendy came down twice again, hard, with the riding crop. The eyes of the mistresses in their chairs lit up. "This is not a high school play!" she said. "You are begging for your very life here, slave, even if you're not aware of it! Now beg, and mean it, or you will feel my whip!"

Tears ran down Alicia's face as she cried, "Oh, please, please, slave, I want your dick in my cunt!" She sobbed loudly. "I want it so badly! Please, slave, give me your dick!"

At a command from Wendy, Leslie obeyed. Standing behind Alicia, she pushed the head of the dildo in; all too late, Alicia realized that the dildo was going into her ass. She screamed with pain as Leslie thrust with her hips and stuck the huge dildo inside.

Oblivious to Alicia's cries, Leslie kept up the rhythm that her teacher had ordered her to do. Tears ran down Alicia's face and she cried out each time the dildo was pushed into her ass. Wendy commanded Leslie to continue, and stepped over to where Ellen watched, horrified. Calmly, Wendy grabbed her by the hair and dragged her to the front of the room.

"I recall seeing you at your mistress' house," Wendy told her. "At that time you really didn't like the other slave your mistress had. You thought that you were better than she. For a while it looked as if it might be true. But in one careless move, you proved yourself wrong."

She motioned for Margot to come over. "Now we will see who is the more obedient slave," she said. "You heard what your partner over there had to say in order to receive the fucking she is now getting. I want to hear the same thing from you."

Ellen was already sobbing ad shaking her head, and the words came out broken but loud enough for Wendy's approval. "Please, slave," she cried, "I want your dick in me! Please stick your dick in me, please, slave!"

Margot had to kneel behind the small slave, but the huge dildo finally found its way into Ellen's poor tight ass. The mistresses in their chairs laughed and jeered at the two slaves who first had to beg their torture from another slave and then endure the huge plastic shafts in their assholes.

Wendy indicated that Brenda should come over, and when she did, she was ordered to stand in front of Alicia, who was still being roughly fucked with the dildo by Leslie.

"Now, Wendy said, "you will beg this particular slave to allow you to suck her cock."

Like Ellen, Alicia could hardly speak for crying, and her words were punctuated by each thrust of the cruel dildo. "Please—slave!" she cried. "Let me—suck—your cock!"

"That was hardly erotic," Wendy said sarcastically, and she lifted the riding crop as a warning.

"Please, slave!" Alicia sobbed. "Please, please, let me suck your cock! Let me take it in my mouth, please!" The mistresses jeered at her and laughed as she strained her neck to reach the tip of the dildo.

"Much better," Wendy smiled, and indicated that Brenda should push the head of the cock within her reach. Once Alicia's lips were around the head of it; however, Brenda was ordered to thrust forward, and Alicia gagged as the whole dildo was stuffed into her mouth. She swallowed hard to regain her composure, but Wendy would not allow the dildo out of her mouth again. Choked with tears, she endured the huge dick in her ass while she licked and sucked obediently at the one strapped to Brenda. What a punishment for a few moments of pleasure! She vowed that never again would she do anything to displease any mistress, no matter how sure she might be of concealing it.

"Now the other one," Wendy said, and Brenda went over to Ellen. The poor little slave, rammed from behind so hard by her slavemate, was also forced to take the huge dildo into her mouth and suck on it lovingly. She too made a vow, to always follow her own slave nature and never be led astray by anyone, no matter how tempting the reward. The punishment was just too severe.

"That will be sufficient," Wendy told Ellen after she had sucked the huge cock for several minutes. Brenda stepped back. Wendy also indicated to Margot and Leslie that they could stop their thrusting. Alicia and Ellen sobbed with pain and relief when the huge dildos were finally taken out of them, and Ellen collapsed on the floor.

"Now go take those off, and prepare yourselves as I told you," Wendy said. The three murmured, "Yes, Mistress," and left the room.

Wendy walked over to her supply wall, while the other mistresses congratulated her on how well she had humiliated the two disobedient slaves.

"It's no wonder you run such a wonderful school, Wendy," Leah said. "You're an expert in putting them in their place."

"You certainly are, Wendy," Anne agreed. "That little scene was just delicious. I'm going to remember that one for a long time."

"I'm glad you enjoyed it," Wendy said, as she found two of the regular, heavy leather classroom collars. "But the best is yet to come."

"We've figured that out," Diane laughed. "We tried to coax it out of Elizabeth when you were gone, but she's as tight-lipped as you are! We can hardly wait."

The regular collars were buckled around Ellen's and Alicia's throats, indicating that once again they were only regular students who had not finished the course. More than the ass-fucking, more than the dildo-sucking, the familiar heavy collars around their throats shamed the two. Their classmates were graduating; they had failed and would be left behind. Wendy then led them to the wall and snapped chains on the collars, fastening the other ends to the steel rings in the wall. Separated from the ceremony, they were forced to watch as another reminder of their momentary indiscretion that would cost them so dearly.

The three slaves returned. Cleaned up, their hair combed, they wore the special velvet collars about their throats and carried their mortarboards in their hands. They stood by the doorway, their eyes down deferentially, awaiting further instructions from the mistress who would not be their teacher much longer.

"You may put those on," Wendy said, and the three obediently adjusted the flat boards on their heads. From their spot chained to the wall, Alicia and Ellen watched with envy. Their physical pain was nothing compared to the shame they now felt.

"I will give these in alphabetical order," Wendy said. "Mistress Anne, will you come up here?" Anne did.

Wendy then called Leslie over, who immediately knelt at her mistress' feet, naked but for the mortarboard and the velvet collar.

"Your slave is a credit to our school," Wendy said. "In her lessons, in her examinations, and in every aspect of her training, she has shown herself to be a slave capable of tending to any need you might have. For this reason I would like to present this proof of her graduation." She shook Anne's hand,

and gave her a parchment diploma rolled and tied with a bright red ribbon. Anne thanked her, then returned to her chair, while Leslie walked over and knelt on the floor at the far side of the room.

"Mistress Leah," Wendy called. Leah came up, and at her teacher's orders, Margot came over and knelt respectfully beside her mistress, a position Leah had believed she would never see.

"This night is one of joy and also disappointment for you, I'm sure," Wendy said. "On the one hand, it is truly a shame that your other slave committed her little indiscretion, for she has the potential to become a superb slave. However, I am confident that with a few more lessons, you will be accepting her diploma as well very shortly. I know that tonight's lesson has made quite an impression on her." Ellen hung her head and sobbed quietly for shaming her mistress before the whole school.

"But you have a great joy here as well," Wendy continued. "I know that when you first brought this slave to me, you were doubtful that she would ever work out.

"Not only did she work out, but she has proven herself to one of the best slaves I have seen in a long time. I know that you will have nothing but satisfaction with this one, and I would like to present you with this proof of graduation."

Again a beribboned scroll was handed over, and Leah shook Wendy's hand, then returned to her chair, while Margot walked over and knelt next to Leslie.

At a hand signal, Brenda came over and knelt before her mistress.

"It seems rather strange that I should be handing out one of these to myself," Wendy said. "But if it hadn't been for this particular slave, there might never have been a school.

"This slave came to me with several bad habits, and I was determined that I wasn't going to put up with them. When I discussed it with Mistress Diane, she mentioned that she had noticed slaves with bad habits as well, and we thought that someone should do something about it. Well, one thing led to another, and that someone turned out to be me."

She picked up the diploma and held it between her hands as if it were her riding crop. "This slave was the first student of the school, and I am proud to say that she completed the course perfectly and has also graduated with honors."

She put the diploma in a drawer of the table, and Brenda walked across the room and knelt beside the other two. There was a round of applause from the floor, and the slaves blushed even though they knew it was not for them, but for their mistresses and for their teacher.

For Alicia and Ellen, there was nothing but misery. They looked at the two diplomas left on the table, beautifully tied with ribbon, that should rightfully have been theirs. They would have been up there, accepting their awards with honor, had they not fallen! Their faces were scarlet with shame and they hung their heads.

"Now," Wendy said, "it's my pleasure to unveil the special honors that you have heard so much about. They will be given to all slaves who graduate from this school!" The two chained to the wall received a swift admonishing look from Wendy before she continued, "And only to those who graduate. If you see a slave with one of there, it means that she has been trained in every aspect of the art of service to a mistress. Almost like a guarantee of quality," she added, and the mistresses laughed at her joke.

Elizabeth handed her a small box, and Wendy stepped over to where the three mistresses sat and opened it. They craned their heads for a look.

"Oh, Wendy, it's marvelous!" Diane said.

"Just gorgeous," Anne agreed.

"You're a genius, Wendy," Leah said. "Only you could have thought up something so beautiful and so special."

Nestled in the box was a gold nipple ring. Although it would have been beautiful on its own, this one was decorated with a tiny gold "W" nestled between two tiny diamonds.

"The 'W' indicates that they have graduated from Mistress Wendy's school," Wendy said. "I hope it will be a continuing reminder of the lessons they have learned and the way they must always serve their mistress—perfection only, nothing less."

"I can assure you that Margot will wear it constantly," Leah said. "Ellen, too—when she graduates." Ellen shrank at her mistress' cold words.

The mistresses discovered that an object pushed into the corner with a cloth thrown over it was actually a folding cot. At Wendy's command, Brenda brought it to the front of the class and unfolded it.

"Again, we will go in alphabetical order," Wendy said. "Mistress Anne, your slave may prepare for her graduation honor."

"On the cot," Anne ordered, and Leslie obediently got on it instantly. Although she was not looking forward to the needle itself, she hoped that it wouldn't be long before one of the gold nipple rings was inserted into her flesh.

Elizabeth opened her bag and laid the tools of her art on the table. She sat beside Leslie, stretched out on the cot, and prepared her by rubbing the area carefully with disinfectant. A regular customer would have had the operation explained to her, and would have been guided through it, but Elizabeth showed no more emotion than a veterinarian preparing to give a dog an injection. The woman on the cot was only a slave, simply property to be pierced, and that was what she was there to do.

Wendy took a moment and glanced at the other two slaves waiting their turn on the floor. Brenda's face was filled with anticipation; she wanted desperately to wear her mistress' nipple ring. Margot's eyes were alive with joy and craving. She wanted the nipple ring too, but she was also longing for the long silver needle that would unhesitatingly slide through her flesh.

Elizabeth checked her equipment and then selected a fine, long-handled pair of forceps with tiny loops at the end. She used these to grasp Leslie's nipple and pull it up. Leslie held her breath and watched, fascinated, as Elizabeth worked.

The long, thin needle was lined up against one of the forceps loops holding the nipple in place. Then, in a graceful, fluid motion, Elizabeth pushed it into the nipple to line up with the loop on the other side.

Leslie flinched for just a moment, but Elizabeth held her nipple firmly. The needle passed smoothly through the flesh, and the whole room—mistresses and slaves alike—watched, fascinated, as Elizabeth pulled it through. Once it was done, she pushed up one of the nipple rings and quickly pushed it through the hole and fastened it. The job was done.

Leslie let out her breath and looked down. The ring was firmly in place, her proof to the world that she had passed her examinations with honor. She didn't think she'd ever seen a more beautiful piece of jewelry.

"Just gorgeous," Anne repeated, and the others nodded.

"Wendy, the first thing I'm doing is going out and showing this to everyone," she continued. Leslie got up off the cot, slightly shaky after her experience, but she quickly regained her composure and walked back to take her place beside Brenda and Margot. "I want everyone to be envious of this. They'll be putting their slaves through your school just so they can get one of these."

"Mistress Leah, your slave next," Wendy said. Leah did not have to give any command to Margot; within seconds she was on her feet, eager to lie down and have her soft nipple pierced by the cold steel.

Everything was switched as the new slave stretched out for her ring; Elizabeth put on fresh gloves, and clean forceps and needle were opened. Once again the nipple was sterilized, but there was no holding of breath this time. Elizabeth squeezed the nipple tightly, and Margot smiled as the cold forceps loops held her flesh firmly.

The sharp tip of the needle pricked her nipple, and Margot almost groaned with pleasure. Then came the strong, sure, fluid movement that drove the needle completely through her. She closed her eyes and sighed ever so quietly, savoring the moment. She wished the piercing could take an hour.

It was over very quickly, however, as Elizabeth inserted the special gold ring and fastened it. Margot walked back over to her spot and knelt. Her nipple was burning and she sat contentedly, enjoying every twinge and discomfort. She only hoped that one day her mistress might decide that a chain on it, perhaps with a small weight on the end, would make a nice decoration occasionally. In her mind's eye, she could see the small ring weighted down, pulling her nipple down with it, and she smiled.

It was Brenda's turn next, and there was a special surprise for her. Since she was not only a student but also the mistress' personal slave, her nipple ring had four diamonds surrounding the "W." Her eyes lit up when Wendy pointed out the difference to the other women, and she thanked her mistress for it profusely.

She longed to wear it, and stretched out eagerly on the cot. Once again the gloves were changed and fresh instruments opened, and Brenda felt the cold forceps grasp her nipple and squeeze.

The needle found its mark and slipped through the warm flesh easily. Once the ring was in place, Brenda admired it, the way the rich gold looked against her skin and the sparkle of the tiny diamonds. She got up and went back to the wall to kneel with the other two.

The mistresses admired them as they knelt, all of them with the gold rings in their right nipples.

"They look lovely on their own, but there's so much you can do with them," Wendy said, as Elizabeth packed the piercing equipment back into her bag. "You can hang chains off them or other jewelry. And if your slave gives you any kind of problem, you can always twist it to get your point across. Except," she added, "I don't expect much problem with this group. If they've graduated, then they're superb slaves."

The two misguided slaves still chained to the wall had completely learned their lesson. To miss the diploma was bad enough, but this! Ellen knew that Margot would wear the ring like a badge in front of her. They were both bitterly disappointed that their breasts were not adorned like the others, and both resolved that they would quickly learn their extra lessons and hopefully win back Mistress Wendy's approval and pass their final examinations again. How they wanted to wear the rings!

The graduation ceremony over, the mistresses retired to the living room, where the three slaves, their nipple rings shining, served them champagne and finally brought out the trays of delicious hors d'oeuvres that had been delivered by the caterer earlier in the day. The women discussed the ceremony while the three slaves stayed nearby, ready to refill an empty glass, take a plate, or bring a clean napkin.

Naturally no one discussed Ellen and Alicia, who remained in the classroom with the lights out, chained to the wall, nursing both their sore asses and their badly wounded pride. They also knew that their lesson had just been a taste of things to come, for both of them had yet to go home and face the wrath of their mistresses for what they had done.

They could hear the party faintly in the living room. Out there, mistresses were smiling and congratulating Wendy and mentioning other mistresses who had already expressed interest in enrolling their slaves as students.

"I filled my next class already," Wendy said. "I may have to have two going at the same time to keep up with the demand. I never dreamed this would be so successful."

"I told you it would," Diane said, smiling over the rim of her champagne glass.

"Well, in a way it is comforting to know that there are so many slaves out there filled with bad habits," Wendy said.

"Why is that?" Leah asked, puzzled. "I thought the whole idea behind setting up your school was because you were tired of slaves with bad habits."

"Oh, they're certainly no fun when they're your

own," Wendy laughed. "But when you get the opportunity to beat those bad habits right out of them—now that's more fun than you can imagine."

"Oh, of course!" Anne said. "And back in that classroom you certainly showed us how well you can do that. Wendy, I'm still all hot and bothered over that little episode."

"Then I have just the thing for you," Wendy said. "We can all check out my new toy. The slaves can clean up in here while we're gone."

"A new toy?" Diane asked, as she put down her glass and got up, following Wendy.

"An inspiration from Anne," Wendy said. "I had a whirlpool installed. I thought it might be interesting whenever we wanted some ... hmm ... good clean fun."

The three mistresses, along with Elizabeth, followed Wendy down the hall to the room where the huge whirlpool was. Ignoring the two slaves who were picking up glasses in the living room, Brenda stood in the hallway.

She knew that very shortly her mistress would call her to bring clean towels and fresh glasses of champagne; her training told her that she would, and her love of her mistress ensured that she would wait patiently until the call came and the order was given.

She touched the gold nipple ring with her finger, and shivered at the burning that went through her from the tender, newly pierced flesh. Then she brought the tip of her finger to her lips and kissed it.

Her mistress would need her, and her mistress would command her. Touching her nipple ring, fingering her velvet collar, Brenda stood in the hallway and waited. The call would come and without fail, at any time, at any place, she would be ready. There simply was no other way.

People are talking about:

The Masquerade Erotic Book Society Newsletter

◆◆◆◆◆◆◆◆◆◆◆◆◆◆◆◆◆◆◆◆

FICTION, ESSAYS, REVIEWS, PHOTOGRAPHY, INTERVIEWS, EXPOSÉS, AND MUCH MORE!

◆◆◆◆◆◆◆◆◆◆◆◆◆◆◆◆◆◆◆◆

"I received the new issue of the newsletter; it looks better and better."
—*Michael Perkins*

"I must say that yours is a nice little magazine, literate and intelligent."
—*HH, Great Britain*

"Fun articles on writing porn and about the peep shows, great for those of us who will probably never step onto a strip stage or behind the glass of a booth, but love to hear about it, wicked little voyeurs that we all are, hm? Yes indeed...."
—*MT, California*

"Many thanks for your newsletter with essays on various forms of eroticism. Especially enjoyed your new Masquerade collections of books dealing with gay sex."
—*GF, Maine*

"... a professional, insider's look at the world of erotica ..."
—*SCREW*

"I recently received a copy of *The Masquerade Erotic Book Society Newsletter*. I found it to be quite informative and interesting. The intelligent writing and choice of subject matter are refreshing and stimulating. You are to be congratulated for a publication that looks at different forms of eroticism without leering or smirking."
—*DP, Connecticut*

"Thanks for sending the books and the two latest issues of *The Masquerade Erotic Book Society Newsletter*. Provocative reading, I must say."
—*RH, Washington*

"Thanks for the latest copy of *The Masquerade Erotic Book Society Newsletter*. It is a real stunner."
—*CJS, New York*

Free GIFT

When you subscribe to:

The Masquerade Erotic Book Society Newsletter

Receive two Masquerade books of your choice.

Please send me TWO MASQUERADE BOOKS FREE!

1. _____

2. _____

☐ I've enclosed my payment of $30.00 for a one-year subscription (six issues) to: **THE MASQUERADE EROTIC BOOK SOCIETY NEWSLETTER.**

Name _____

Address _____

_____ Apt. # _____

City _____ State _____ Zip _____

Tel. ( ) _____

Payment: ☐ Check ☐ Money Order ☐ Visa ☐ MC

Card No. _____

Exp. Date _____

Please allow 4–6 weeks delivery. No C.O.D. orders. Please make all checks payable to Masquerade Books, 801 Second Avenue, N.Y., N.Y., 10017. Payable in U.S. currency only.

THE MASQUERADE

ROSEBUD BOOKS — $4.95

PASSAGE AND OTHER STORIES
Aarona Griffin

An S/M romance. In the title story, lovely Nina was frightened away from her lesbian passions at an early age, and was now leading a "safe" life, until she finds herself infatuated with a woman she spots at a local café. One night Nina follows her and finds herself enmeshed in an endless maze leading not only to her object of passion, but to a mysterious world where women test the edges of sexuality and power. **3057-1**

DISTANT LOVE & OTHER STORIES
A.L. Reine

In the title story, Leah Michaels and her lover Ranelle have had four years of blissful smoldering passion together. One night, when Ranelle is out of town, Leah records an audio "Valentine," a cassette filled with erotic reminiscences of their life together in vivid, pulsating detail. As she continues, Leah finds herself becoming more and more excited, more and more turned on! **3056-3**

PROVINCETOWN SUMMER
Lindsay Welsh

Pure lesbian libido explodes in this book of short stories written by and about the sisters of Sappho. This completely original collection is devoted exclusively to white-hot desire between women. In the title story, a writer shares a passionate but impossible love with an artist in a sleepy seaside town. From the casual encounters of women on the prowl to the enduring erotic bond between old lovers, the women of *Provincetown Summer* will set your senses on fire! **3040-7**

EROTIC *PLAYGIRL* ROMANCES

THE COMPLETE *PLAYGIRL* FANTASIES

The very best—and very hottest—women's fantasies are collected here, fresh from the pages of *Playgirl*. These knockouts from the infamous "Reader's Fantasy Forum" prove, once again, that truth can indeed be hotter, wilder, and *better* than fiction. **3075-X**

DREAM CRUISE
Gwenyth James

Angelia has it all—a brilliant career and a beautiful face to match. But she longs to kick up her high heels and have some fun, so she takes an island vacation and vows to leave her sexual inhibitions behind. From the moment her plane takes off, she finds herself in one hot and steamy encounter after another, and her horny holiday doesn't end on Monday morning! **3045-8**

EROTIC LIBRARY

RHINOCEROS BOOKS $6.95

EVIL COMPANIONS *Michael Perkins*
A handsome edition of this cult classic that includes a new preface by Samuel R. Delany. Set in New York City during the tumultuous waning years of the 60s, *Evil Companions* has been hailed as "a frightening classic." A young couple explore the nether reaches of the erotic unconscious in a shocking confrontation with the extremes of passion. *Evil Companions* is, unquestionably, a dark and compelling jewel. **3067-9**

THE SECRET RECORD *Michael Perkins*
Rhino*ceros* is proud to present the paperback edition of this landmark work on erotic literature. Michael Perkins, a renowned author and critic of sexually explicit fiction, surveys the field with authority and unique insight. Updated and revised to include the latest trends, tastes, and developments in this much-misunderstood genre, *The Secret Record* is the last word on this most controversial of subjects. **3039-3**

TOURNIQUET *Alice Joanou*
"Remember," she said, "you were my father's pet, and now you are reduced again as my slave until I feel you are worthy to service my pleasure. For now you are my valet, my whipping post, and, if the whim takes me, an object that fills my needs. Now kiss me and beg for forgiveness." At which the slave kissed her extended hand and dropped to his knees. **3067-9**

CANNIBAL FLOWER *Alice Joanou*
"She is waiting in her darkened bedroom, as she has waited throughout history, to seduce and ultimately destroy the men who are foolish enough to be blinded by her irresistible charms. She is Salome, Lucrezia Borgia, Delilah—endlessly alluring, the fulfillment of your every desire. She will ensnare, entrap, and drive her willing victims to the cutting edge of ecstasy—and then devour them. She is the goddess of sexuality, and *Cannibal Flower* is her haunting siren song."—Michael Perkins **72-6**

ILLUSIONS *Daniel Vian*
Two surreal, disturbing tales of danger and desire on the eve of World War II. From private homes to lurid cafés to decaying streets, passion is explored, exposed, and placed in stark contrast to the brutal violence of the time. *Illusions* peels the frightened mask from the face of desire, and studies its changing features under the dim lights of a lonely Berlin evening. **3074-1**

MY DARLING DOMINATRIX *Grant Antrews*
When a man and a woman fall in love it's supposed to be simple, uncomplicated, easy—unless that woman happens to be a dominatrix. This unpretentious love story captures the richness and depth of this very special kind of love. Devoid of sleaze or shame, this is an honest and heartbreaking story of the power and passion that binds human beings together. **3055-5**

LOVE IN WARTIME *Liesel Kulig*
Madeleine knew that the handsome SS officer was a dangerous man. But she was just a cabaret singer in Nazi-occupied Paris, trying to survive in a perilous time. When Josef fell in love with her, he discovered that a beautiful, intelligent, and amoral woman can sometimes be even more dangerous than the fiercest warrior. **3044-X**

ALL MASQUERADE BOOKS $4.95 EACH

HELOISE *Sarah Jackson*
A panoply of sensual tales harkening back to the golden age of Victorian erotica. Desire is examined in all its intricacy, as fantasies are explored and unavoidable urges explode. Innocence meets experience time and again in these passionate stories dedicated to the pleasures of the body. Sweetly torrid! **3073-3**

MASTER OF TIMBERLAND *Sara H. French*
"Welcome to Timberland Resort," he began. "We are delighted that you have come to serve us. And you may all be assured that we will require service of you in the strictest sense. We demand and we will have only the most complete, unquestioning, uncomplaining, immediate obedience. Infractions will be punished quickly and severely, as you have seen. Our discipline is the most demanding in the world. You will be trained here by the best. You can always be proud that you were chosen. And now your new Masters will make their choices." **3059-8**

GARDEN OF DELIGHT *Sydney St. James*
A vivid account of sexual awakening that follows an innocent but insatiably curious young woman's journey from the furtive, forbidden joys of dormitory life to the unabashed carnality of the wild world. Pretty Pauline blossoms with each new experiment in the sensual arts. **3058-X**

STASI SLUT *Anthony Bobarzynski*
Innocent Adina longs to escape her provincial middle-class life. There's only one problem: Adina lives in East Germany under the iron-fisted Communist government, far from the sexually liberated, uninhibited debauchery of the West. When she meets a group of ruthless and corrupt STASI agents, she recognizes them as her only outlet for freedom. The agents use Adina as a pawn in their political chess game as well as for their own gratification until she makes a final bid for total freedom in the revolutionary climax of this *Red*-hot thriller! **3052-0**

BLUE TANGO *Hilary Manning*
Ripe and tempting Julie is haunted by the sounds of extraordinary passion beyond her bedroom wall. Alone at night she fantasizes about taking part in the amorous dramas of her hosts, Claire and Edward. When she finds a way to watch the nightly debauch as well as listen, her insatiable curiosity put to full-blown lust and her fantasy becomes flesh. **3037-7**

THE APPLICANT *Lizbeth Dusseau*
"Adventuresome young woman who enjoys being submissive sought by married couple in early forties. Expect no limits." Hilary answers an ad, hoping to find someone who can meet her special needs. The beautiful Liza turns out to be a flawless mistress, and together with her husband Oliver, she trains Hilary to be the perfect servant. **3038-5**

SEDUCTIONS *Sincerity Jones*
Twelve short stories of erotic encounters, told with a woman's sensibility. This original collection includes couplings of every variety, including a woman who helps fulfill her man's fantasy of making it with another man, a dangerous liaison in the back of a taxi, an uncommon alliance between a Wall Street type and a funky downtown woman, and a walk on the wild side for a vacationing sexual adventurer. Thoroughly modern women! **83-1**

ALL MASQUERADE BOOKS $4.95 EACH

THE CATALYST *Sara Adamson*
The forbidden world of SM is explored in this story of initiation and discovery. After viewing a controversial, explicitly kinky film full of images of bondage and submission, several audience members find themselves deeply moved by the erotic suggestions they've seen on the screen. A lesbian couple spank and make up after a heated argument. Two gay men pick up a leatherman to help them re-enact their favorite scenes from the film. A suburban married couple break out the rope and engage in a drama of surrender and control. These are just a few of the first-time experiments set off by *The Catalyst*! **3015-6**

LUST *Palmiro Vicarion*
A wealthy and powerful man of leisure recounts his rise up the corporate ladder and his corresponding descent into debauchery. Adventure and political intrigue provide a stimulating backdrop for this tale of a classic scoundrel with an uncurbed appetite for sexual power! **82-3**

WAYWARD *Peter Jason*
A mysterious countess hires a bus and tour guide for an unusual vacation. Traveling through Europe's most notorious cities and resorts, the bus picks up the countess' friends, lovers, and acquaintances from every walk of life in pursuit of unbridled sensual pleasure. Each guest brings unique sexual tastes and talents to the group, climaxing in countless orgies, outrageous acts, and endless deviation! **3004-0**

ASK ISADORA *Isadora Alman*
Six years of collected columns on sex and relationships. Alman has been called a hip Dr. Ruth and a sexy Dear Abby. Her advice is sharp, funny, and pertinent to anyone experiencing the delights and dilemmas of being a sexual creature in today's perplexing world. **61-0**

LOUISE BELHAVEL

FRAGRANT ABUSES
The sex saga of Clara and Iris continues as the now-experienced girls enjoy themselves with a new circle of worldly friends whose imaginations definitely match their own. Against an exotic array of locations, Clara and Iris sample the unique delights of every country and its culture! **88-2**

DEPRAVED ANGELS
The third and final installment in the incredible adventures of Clara and Iris. Together with their friends, lovers, and worldly acquaintances, Clara and Iris explore the frontiers of depravity at home and abroad. Their scandalous sexcapades delight and intrigue everyone, and their natural curiosity and sweet, sexy personalities guarantee that there will always be new and exotic thrills for them to experience just over the next horizon! **92-0**

TITIAN BERESFORD

CINDERELLA
A magical exploration of the full erotic potential of this fairy tale. Titian Beresford triumphs again with castle dungeons and tightly corseted ladies-in-waiting, naughty viscounts and impossibly cruel masturbatrixes—nearly every conceivable method of erotic torture is explored and described in lush, vivid detail. A fetishist's dream and a masochist's delight! **3024-5**

JUDITH BOSTON

Young Edward would have been lucky to get the stodgy old companion he thought his parents had hired for him. Instead, an exqusite woman arrives at his door, and from the top of her tightly-wound bun to the tips of her impossibly high heels, Judith Boston is in complete control. Naughty Edward's compulsively lewd behavior never goes unpunished by the severe Judith Boston! **87-4**

NINA FOXTON

A young aristocrat finds herself bored by the run-of-the-mill amusements for ladies of good breeding. Instead of taking tea with gentlemen, outrageous Nina invents a device to "milk" them of their most private essences. No one says "no" to Nina! **71-8**

CHINA BLUE

KUNG FU NUNS

"When I could stand the pleasure no longer, she lifted me out of the chair and sat me down on top of the table. She then lifted her skirt. The sight of her perfect legs clad in white stockings and a petite garter belt further mesmerized me. I lean particularly towards white garter belts." **3031-8**

SECRETS OF THE CITY **03-3**

HARRIET DAIMLER

DARLING • INNOCENCE

Two great erotic novels. In *Darling*, a virgin is raped by a mugger. Driven by her urge for revenge, she searches New York for him in a furious sexual hunt that leads to rape and murder. In *Innocence,* a young invalid determines to experience sex through her voluptuous nurse. Extraordinary erotic imagination! **3047-4**

THE PLEASURE THIEVES

They come in the night, cleaning out the contents of the safe while the orgy rages downstairs. They are the Pleasure Thieves, Harry and Philip, a pair of ex-cellmates and lovers whose sexually preoccupied targets are set up by luscious Carol Stoddard, the publisher of *Femme* magazine. She forms an ultra-hot sexual threesome with them, trying every combination from two-on-ones to daisy chains—because pleasures are even sweeter when they're stolen! **036-X**

AKBAR DEL PIOMBO

DUKE COSIMO

A kinky, lighthearted romp of non-stop action is played out against the boudoirs, ballrooms, and bathrooms of the European nobility, who seem to do nothing all day except each other. From stable boys to scullery maids, princes to prostitutes, everyone takes part in this orgiastic celebration of the *crème de la crème* of society! **3052-0**

A CRUMBLING FAÇADE

The return of that incorrigible rogue, Henry Pike, last seen deflowering maidens and ruining proper ladies in *Paula*. Pike continues his pursuit of sex, fair or otherwise, in the most elegant homes of the most irreproachable and debauched aristocrats. Their incessant orgies, flagrant gropings, and most public indiscretions are sure to stimulate even the most jaded appetites. **3043-1**

PAULA
A brilliant, witty novel of unabashed sexual excess: "How bad do you want me?" she asked again, her voice husky, breathy. I shrank back, for my desire for her was swelling to unspeakable proportions. "Turn around," she said, and I obeyed, willing then to do as she asked. **3036-9**

ROBERT DESMOND

PROFESSIONAL CHARMER
A dissolute gigolo lives a parasitical life of luxury by providing his sexual services to the rich and bored. Traveling in the most exclusive social circles, this gun-for-hire will gratify the lewdest and most vulgar cravings in exchange for nothing more than a fine meal or a shred of stylish clothing. Each and every exploit he must perform is described in lurid detail in this story of a prostitute's progress! **3003-2**

THE SWEETEST FRUIT
Connie Lashfield is determined to seduce and destroy pious Father Chadcroft to show her former lover that she no longer requires his sexual services. She corrupts the priest into forsaking all that he holds sacred, destroys his peaceful parish, and slyly manipulates him with her smoldering looks and hypnotic sexual aura. **95-5**

MICHAEL DRAX

SILK AND STEEL
"He stood tall and strong in the inky shadows of her room, and Akemi lifted up on her pallet to see the man better, hardly able to believe her luck. Although the man didn't speak a word, Akemi knew what he was there for. He let his robe fall to the floor. Akemi could offer no resistance as the shadowy figure knelt before her, gazing down upon her. Why would she resist? This was what she wanted all along...." **3032-6**

OBSESSIONS
Gorgeous, haughty Victoria is determined to become a top model, using her special abilities to sexually ensnare the powerful men and women who control the fashion industry: the rich voyeur who enjoys photographing Victoria almost as much as she enjoys teasing him; Paige, who finds herself compelled to witness Victoria's conquests; Pietro and Alex, who take turns and then join in for a sizzling threesome. **3012-1**

JOCELYN JOYCE

CAROUSEL
It is Paris in the Twenties. A young American woman, Hilary Blair, leaves her husband when she discovers he is having an affair with their maid. She then becomes the sexual plaything of various Parisian voluptuaries. Wild sex, low morals, and ultimate decadence in the flamboyant years before the European collapse. **3051-2**

SABINE
Sabine. One of the most unforgettable seductresses ever to appear on the printed page. There is no man or woman who can refuse her once she casts her spell. And once ensnared, no lover can do anything less than give up his whole life for her. Great men and empires fall at her feet; but she is haughty, distracted, impervious. It is the eve of WW II, and Sabine must find a new lover equal to her talents and her tastes. **3046-6**

THREE WOMEN
A web of sexual power and dependence ties three beautiful women to each other and the men who love them. Dr. Helen Webber finds that her natural authority thrills and excites her high-powered lover Aaron. His daughter Jan is involved in a scorching affair with a married man whose society wife eases her loneliness by slumming at the local watering hole with the regulars. A torrid, tempestuous triangle! **3025-3**

THE WILD HEART
A luxury hotel is the setting for this artful web of sex, desire, and love. A newlywed wife sees sex as a conjugal duty, while her hungry husband tries to awaken her. A ripe Parisian entertains the wealthy guests for the love of money. A delicious variation on the old Inn-and-out! **3007-5**

DEMON HEAT
An ancient vampire stalks the unsuspecting in the form of a beautiful woman. Unlike the legendary Dracula, this fiend doesn't drink blood; she craves a different kind of potion. When her insatiable appetite has drained every last drop of juice from her victims, she leaves them spent and hungering for more—even if it means being sucked to death! **79-3**

HAREM SONG
Young, sensuous Amber flees her cruel uncle and provincial English village in search of a better life, but finds she is no match for the glittering lights and mean streets of London. Soon Amber becomes a classy call girl and is eventually sold into a lusty Sultan's harem—a vocation for which she possesses more than average talent! **73-4**

JADE EAST
Laura, passive and passionate, follows her domineering husband Emilio to Hong Kong. He gives her to Wu Li, a Chinese connoisseur of sexual perversions, who passes her on to Madeleine, a flamboyant lesbian. Madeleine's friends make Laura the centerpiece in Hong Kong's underground orgies. As she is being taken by three men while the guests watch, Laura sees Emilio with a beautiful, dark-haired girl: He is about to start another on her downward path. A journey into sexual slavery! **60-2**

RAWHIDE LUST
Diana Beaumont, the young wife of a U.S. Marshal, is kidnapped as an act of vengeance against her husband. Jack Beaumont sets out on a long journey to get his wife back, but finally catches up with her trail only to learn that she's been sold into white slavery in Mexico. A story of the Old West, when the only law was made by the gun, and a woman's virtue was often worth no more than the price of a few steers! **55-6**

THE JAZZ AGE
This is an erotic novel of life in the Roaring Twenties. A Wall Street attorney becomes suspicious of his mistress while his wife has an interlude with a lesbian lover. *The Jazz Age* is a romp of erotic realism in the heyday of the flapper and the speakeasy. **48-3**

ALIZARIN LAKE

MISS HIGH HEELS
It was a delightful punishment few men dared to dream of. Who could have predicted how far it would go? Forced by his wicked sisters to dress and behave like a proper lady, Dennis Beryl finds he enjoys life as Denise much more! This story of sensuous penalties, wild pleasures, and unexpected switches will surely give life to the fairy tale fantasies that lie behind the most private desires.... **3066-0**

CELESTE
Traveling through Europe, two women and a man try everything and everyone on their horny holiday. None of them are afraid of trying anything new or different, including each other! **75-0**

RED DOG SALOON
Bella Denburg took a vow to avenge her cousin Genevieve, who was kidnapped and raped by Quantrill's Raiders. Bella intended to get herself accepted as a camp follower of Quantrill, find the men responsible, and kill them. Her pursuit led her through whorehouses, rapes, and terrible violence until at last she held each of the guilty ones, unsuspecting, between her legs. Lust and revenge! **68-8**

PASSION IN RIO
For four days and nights during the great Carnival, when all sexual inhibitions are temporarily cast aside, Rio de Janiero goes mad. For lesbian designer Kay Arnold, it begins when the lovely junior designer who accompanies her returns her kiss. For Roger and Lucille Porter, the carnival begins when they learn from celebrating Brazilians how to satisfy each other. The world's most frenzied sexual fiesta! **54-8**

THE KING OF PLEASURE
Stanton Ames has delved deeper into the sexual arts than ordinary men dream of. Beginning with his early initiation at the hands at the hands of Fraulien Schneider and throughout his career in the publishing world he sought beautiful masochists who longed for the ecstasy he could bring them. Strong stuff! **45-9**

LUST OF THE COSSACKS
The countess enjoys watching beautiful peasant girls submit to her perverse lesbian manias. She tutors her only male lover in the joys of erotic torture and in return he lures a beautiful ballerina to her estate, where he intends to present her to the countess as a plaything. Painful pleasures! **41-6**

TURKISH DELIGHTS
During WW I, the Turks exercised unbelievable sexual sadism against the Greek women guerrillas and English spies who fell into their hands. "With a roar of triumph, Kemil Chokar gripped the girl's breasts and forced her back upon the thick rug on the floor.... He went at her like a bull, buffeting her mercilessly, and she groaned ... to her own amazement, with ecstasy!" **40-8**

POOR DARLINGS
Here are the impressions and feelings, the excitement and lust, that young women feel when they submit to desire. Not just with male partners—but with women too. Desperate, gasping, scandalous sex! **33-5**

THE LUSTFUL TURK
A young bride, just entering the bloom of womanhood is captured by Tunisian pirates and held for ransom in a harem. There she was sexually broken in by crazed eunuchs, corrupted by lesbian slave girls, and then given to the queen as a sexual toy. Turkish lust unleashed! **28-9**

CAPTIVE MAIDENS   **3014-8**
SLAVE ISLAND   **3006-7**

MARY LOVE

NAUGHTIER AT NIGHT
"He wanted to seize her. Her buttocks under the tight suede material were absolutely succulent—carved and molded. What attracted him most was her lovely face—her deep blue eyes, her nose, and especially her smile. What on earth had he done to deserve a morsel of a girl like this?" **3030-X**

THE INSTRUMENTS OF THE PASSION
All that remains is the diary of a young initiate, detailing the twisted rituals of a mysterious cult institution known only as "Rossiter." Behind sinister walls, a beautiful young woman performs an unending drama of pain and humiliation. What is the impulse that justifies her, night after night, in consenting to this strange ceremony? And to what lengths will her aberrant passion drive her? **3010-5**

TUTORED IN LUST
This tale of the initiation and instruction of a carnal college co-ed and her fellow students unlocks the sex secrets of the classroom. Books take a back seat to secret societies and their bizarre ceremonies in this story of students with an unquenchable thirst for knowledge! **78-5**

FESTIVAL OF VENUS
Brigeen Mooney fled her home in the west of Ireland to avoid being forced into a nunnery. But her refuge in Dublin turned out to be dedicated to a different religion. The women she met there belonged to the Old Religion, devoted to sex and sacrifices. They were competing to become sexual priestesses on the Isle of Man. The sex ceremonies of pagan gods! **37-8**

PAUL LITTLE

THE DISCIPLINE OF ODETTE
Odette's family was harsh, but not even whippings and public humiliation could keep her from Jacques, her lover. She was sure marriage to him would rescue her from her family's "corrections." To her horror, she discovers that Jacques, too, has been raised on discipline. **3033-4**

ALL THE WAY
Two excruciating novels from Paul Little in one hot volume! *Going All the Way* features an unhappy man, Jean-Paul, who tries to purge himself of the memory of his lover with a series of quirky and uninhibited women. *Pushover* tells the story of a serial spanker and his celebrated exploits in California. **3023-7**

SLAVES OF CAMEROON
This sordid tale is about the women who were used by German officers for salacious profit. These women were forced to become whores for the German army in this African colony. The most perverse forms of erotic gratification are depicted in this unsavory tale! **3026-1**

THE PRISONER
Judge Black has built a secret room below a women's penitentiary, where he sentences the prisoners to hours of exhibition and torment while his friends watch from their luxurious box seats. Judge Black's House of Corrections is equipped with every kind of device and tool, exquisitely crafted with one purpose in mind: to administer his own brand of rough justice! **3011-3**

THE AUTOBIOGRAPHY OF A FLEA III
That incorrigible voyeur, the Flea, returns for yet another tale of outrageous acts and indecent behavior. This time Flea returns to Provence to spy on the younger generation, now just coming into their own ripe, juicy maturity. With the same wry wit and eye for lurid detail, the Flea's secret observations won't fail to titillate yet again! **94-7**

END OF INNOCENCE
The early days of Women's Emancipation are the setting for this story of some very independent ladies. These girls were willing to go to any lengths to fight for their sexual freedom, and willing to endure any punishment in their desire for total liberation. You've come a long way, baby! **77-7**

VICE PARK PLACE

Rich, lonely divorcée Penelope Luckner drinks alone every night, fending off the advances of sexual suitors that she secretly craves. Alone, she dreams of a lover who can melt her frigid façade. Then she meets Robbie, a much younger man with a virgin's aching appetites, and together they embark on an affair that breaks all their fantasies wide open! **3008-3**

MASTERING MARY SUE

Mary Sue is a rich nymphomaniac whose husband is determined to pervert her, declare her mentally incompetent, and gain control of her fortune. He brings her to a castle in Europe, where a sadistic psychiatrist and his well-trained servants amuse themselves. To Mary Sue's delight, they have stumbled on an unimaginably depraved sex cult, where panting men and women suffer and every kind of corruption is practiced! **3005-9**

WANDA   **3002-4**
ANGELA   **76-9**

ALEXANDER TROCCHI

WHITE THIGHS

A dark fantasy of sexual obsession from a modern erotic master. This is the story of young Saul and his sexual fixation on beautiful, tormented Anna of the white thighs. Their scorching, dangerous passion leads to murder and madness every time they submit. Saul must possess her again and again, no matter what or who stands in his way. A disturbing masterpiece! **3009-1**

SCHOOL FOR SIN

When Peggy leaves the harsh morality of her Irish country home behind for Dublin, her sensuous nature leads to her seduction by a stranger. He recruits her into a training school and she embarks on an education in pleasure. No one knows what awaits them at graduation, but each student is sure to be well schooled in sex! **89-0**

MY LIFE AND LOVES (THE 'LOST' VOLUME)

What happens when you try to fake a sequel to the most scandalous autobiography of the 20th century? If the "forger" is one of the most important figures in modern erotica, you get a masterpiece, and *this is it!* **52-1**

THONGS

"Spain is the land of passion and of death and this death would not have called for further comment had it not been for one striking fact. The naked woman had met her end in a way he had never seen before—a way that had enormous sexual significance. My God, she had been ..." **46-7**

THE CARNAL DAYS OF HELEN SEFERIS

Private Investigator Harvest is determined to find and save Helen Seferis, a beautiful Australian who has been abducted in Algiers. Following clues in Helen's explicit diary he descends into the depths of the white slave trade. Through exotic slave markets, forbidden harems, and sadistic rites he pursues Helen, the ultimate sexual prize! **35-1**

MARCUS VAN HELLER

ADAM & EVE

Adam and Eve long to escape their dull lives by achieving stardom—she in the theater, and he in the art world. Eve soon finds herself acting cozy on the casting couch, while Adam must join a bizarre sex cult to further his artistic career. Everyone has their price in this electrifying tale of ambition and desire! **93-9**

KIDNAP

Nick Harding is called in to investigate a mysterious kidnapping case involving the rich and powerful in London, France, and Geneva. Along the way he has the pleasure of "interrogating" a sensuous exotic dancer named Jeanne and a beautiful English reporter, as he finds himself further enmeshed in the sleazy international crime underworld. A sizzling mystery of sexual intrigue and betrayal!
90-4

LUSCIDIA WALLACE

FOR SALE BY OWNER

Susie Quinten was overwhelmed by the lavishness of the yacht, the glamour of the guests who arrived for the exclusive party. But she didn't know the plans Anthony Douglas and his cohorts had for her—training and sale into slavery. How many sweet young women were taught the pleasures of service in this floating prison? And how many gave as much delight as the newly wicked Susie?
3064-4

THE ICE MAIDEN

Edward Canton has ruthlessly seized everything he wants in life, with one exception: Rebecca Esterbrook. Frustrated by his inability to seduce her with money, he kidnaps her and whisks her away to his remote island compound, where she learns to shed her inhibitions and accept caresses from both men and women. Fully aroused for the first time in her life, she becomes his writhing, red-hot love slave!
3001-6

KATY'S AWAKENING

Poor Katy thinks she's been rescued by a kindly young couple after a terrible car wreck. Little does she suspect that she's been ensnared by a ring of swingers whose tastes run to domination and wild sex parties. Katy becomes the newest initiate into this private club, and she learns the rules from every player!
74-2

MASQUERADE READERS

THE COMPLETE EROTIC READER

The very best in erotic writing—from the scandalous to the sublime—come together in a wicked collection sure to stimulate even the most jaded and "sophisticated" palates. All inhibitions are surrrendered, and no desire is left unflaunted in these steamy celebrations of the body erotic.
3063-6

THE VELVET TONGUE

An orgy of oral gratification! *The Velvet Tongue* celebrates the most mouth-watering, lip-smacking, tongue-twisting action. A feast of fellatio and succulent *soixant-neuf* awaits at this steamy suck-fest.
3029-6

DOUBLE NOVEL ($6.95)

Two novels of illicit desire, combined into one spellbinding volume! *Lisette Joyaux* tells the story of an innocent young woman seduced by a group of beautiful and experienced lesbians who initiate her into a new world of pleasure. *The Story of Monique* explores an underground society's clandestine rituals and scandalous encounters that beckon to the ripe and willing.
86-6

A MASQUERADE READER

Masquerade presents a salacious selection of excerpts from its library of erotica. Infamously strict lessons are learned at the hand of *The English Governess* and *Nina Foxton,* where the notorious Nina proves herself a very harsh taskmistress. Scandalous confessions are to be found in *The Diary of an Angel,* and the harrowing story of a woman whose desires drove her to the ultimate sacrifice in *Thongs* completes this collection.
84-X

INTIMATE PLEASURES

Try a tempting morsel of the forbidden liaisons in *The Prodigal Virgin* and *Eveline,* or the bizarre public displays of carnality in *The Gilded Lily* and *The Story of Monique,* or the insatiable cravings in *The Misfortunes of Mary* and *Darling/Innocence.* Every forbidden desire is flaunted, every inhibition surrendered in these six savory samples! **38-6**

LAVENDER ROSE

A classic collection of lesbian literature: From the writings of Sappho, the queen of the women-lovers of ancient Greece, whose debaucheries on her island have remained infamous for all time, to the turn-of-the-century *Black Book of Lesbianism*; from *Tips to Maidens* to *Crimson Hairs*, a recent lesbian saga—here are the great lesbian writings and revelations. Sappho herself would be turned on! **30-0**

EASTERN EROTICA

DEVA DASI

Dedicated to the cult of the Dasis, the sacred women of India who dedicated their lives to the fulfillment of the senses, this book reveals the secret sexual rites of Shiva. It follows the apprenticeship of a young mistress of the Dancing God, showing sexual practices unknown, undiscovered in the West. The secrets of the craft of sex that will set you on fire! Erotic beyond Western imagination! **29-7**

HOUSES OF JOY

A masterpiece of China's splendid erotic literature. This book is based on the *Ching P'ing Mei*, banned many times. Despite its frequent suppression, it has somehow managed to survive—read it and see why! **51-3**

KAMA HOURI

Ann Pemberton, daughter of the British regimental commander in India, runs away with her servant. Forced to live in a harem, Ann accepts her sexual submission and offers herself to any warrior who wishes to mount her. The natives kindle a fire within her and Ann, sexually ablaze, becomes a legend as the white sex-bitch of the Raj! **39-4**

THE CLASSIC COLLECTION

MAN WITH A MAID

The adventures of Jack and Alice have delighted readers for eight decades! A classic of its genre, *Man with a Maid* tells an outrageous tale of desire, revenge, and submission that is bound to keep yet another generation of readers breathless. **3065-2**

MAN WITH A MAID II

Jack's back! With the assistance of the perverse Alice, he embarks again on a trip through every erotic extreme. Jack leaves no one unsatisfied—least of all, himself, and Alice is always certain to outdo herself in her capacity to corrupt and control. No virtue is safe with these two on the prowl! An incendiary sequel **3071-7**

MAN WITH A MAID: The Conclusion

The final chapter in the classic saga of lust and domination that has thrilled readers for decades. Jack and his willful wife Alice seek out new prey to suffer the pleasures and delights of the Snuggery. The adulterous sister who is corrected with enthusiasm and the clumsy maid who receives grueling guidance are just two who benefit from the lessons learned under the lash and paddle! **3013-X**

THE YELLOW ROOM

Two complete erotic masterpieces. The "yellow room" holds the secrets of lust, lechery, and the lash. There, bare-bottomed, spread-eagled, and open to the world, demure Alice Darvell soon learns to love her lickings from her perverted guardian. Even more exciting is the second torrid tale of hot heiress Rosa Coote and her adventures in punishment and pleasure with her two sexy, sadistic servants, Jane and Jemima. Feverishly erotic! **96-3**

THE BOUDOIR

Masquerade presents a new edition of the classic Victorian magazine, including several bawdy novellas, ribald stories, and indecent anecdotes to arouse and delight. Six volumes of this original journal of indiscretion are presented here in all their salacious glory. Good old-fashioned smut! **85-8**

A WEEKEND VISIT

"Dear Jack, Can you come down for a long weekend visit and amuse three lonely females? I am writing at mother's suggestion. Do come!" Fresh from his erotic exploits in *Man with a Maid*, randy Jack is at it again! **59-9**

THE ENGLISH GOVERNESS

When Lord Lovell's son was expelled from his prep school for masturbation, his father hired a very proper governess to tutor theboy—giving her strict instructions not to spare the rod to break him of his bad habits. But governess Harriet Marwood was addicted to domination. The whip was her loving instrument, and with it she taught young Richard to use the rod in ways he had never dreamed. The downward path to perversion! **43-2**

PLEASURES AND FOLLIES

The exploits of a libertine: "I got astride her, rode her roughshod, plied the crop.... Ashamed by these excesses provoked by my reading, I compiled a well-seasoned Erotikon and it excited me to such a degree that I ... well, pick up my book and see whether it has a similar effect upon you." **26-2**

STUDENTS OF PASSION

When she arrives at the prestigious Beauchamp Academy, Francine is young, innocent, and eager to learn. Her teachers and schoolmates enroll her in a course devoted to passion, anatomy, and lust ... and she's determined to graduate with honors. **22-X**

SACRED PASSIONS

Young Augustus comes into the heavenly sanctuary seeking protection from the enemies of his debt-ridden father. Soon he discovers that the joys of the body far surpass those of the spirit. **21-1**

THE NUNNERY TALES

The Abbess forces her rites of sexual initiation on any maiden who falls into her hands. After exposure to the Mother Superior and her lustful nuns, sweet Emilie, Louise, and the other novices are sexual novices no longer. Cloistered concubinage! **20-3**

FRUITS OF PASSION

From his initiation into endless orgiastic delights by the chambermaid sisters Rose and Manette, the Count de Leon continues his erotic diary for forty years, ending in his Caribbean voyages with the two most uninhibited Victorian Venuses he has ever known. A life totally dedicated to sex! **05-X**

THE EDITORS OF *PLAYGIRL*

MORE *PLAYGIRL* FANTASIES

The editors of *Playgirl* bring you more of their favorites from the "Readers' Fantasy Forum." This collection is even hotter than the last, as the readers of *Playgirl* share their most intimate fantasy encounters, revealing every steamy detail—daydreams only *Playgirl* readers could pen! **69-6**

A Very Special Offer
For a Limited Time Only!

Masquerade Books is proud to present a volume of unparalleled artistry in the field of erotica. *The Journal of Erotica, Volume One* is unquestionably the most stunning collection of erotic art, writing, and photography to be published in the last 30 years.

This sturdy, handsomely bound and embossed volume includes incisive, entertaining fiction and over 80 pages of provocative photography (including 43 full-color plates). From some of the earliest sexual images ever exposed on film (circa 1855), to the seductive, streetwise, and very contemporary work of Katarina Jebb, *The Journal of Erotica* is a feast for the eyes.

The Journal of Erotica will surely be regarded as the most unique and collectible publication since *Eros* burst on the scene in the 60s. No erotic library is complete without it; no afficionado will want to miss it.

The Journal of Erotica, Volume One is available to you for $25.00 a copy (plus $2.50 shipping & handling). Order for yourself or as a holiday gift—but order now! Only a limited number are available. Call toll-free: 1-800-458-9640.

THE MASQUERADE LIBRARY

SECRETS OF THE CITY	03-3	$4.95
FRUITS OF PASSION	05-X	$4.95
ANNABEL FANE	08-4	$4.95
THE FURTHER ADVENTURES OF MADELEINE	04-1	$4.95
THE GILDED LILY	25-4	$4.95
PLEASURES AND FOLLIES	26-2	$4.95
STUDENTS OF PASSION	22-X	$4.95
THE NUNNERY TALES	20-3	$4.95
THE LUSTFUL TURK	28-9	$4.95
DEVA-DASI	29-7	$4.95
THE STORY OF MONIQUE	42-4	$4.95
THE ENGLISH GOVERNESS	43-2	$4.95
POOR DARLINGS	33-5	$4.95
DANCE HALL GIRLS	44-0	$4.95
LAVENDER ROSE	30-0	$4.95
KAMA HOURI	39-4	$4.95
THONGS	46-7	$4.95
THE PLEASURE THIEVES	36-X	$4.95
SACRED PASSIONS	21-1	$4.95
THE CARNAL DAYS OF HELEN SEFERIS	35-1	$4.95
LUST OF THE COSSACKS	41-6	$4.95
THE JAZZ AGE	48-3	$4.95
MY LIFE AND LOVES (THE 'LOST' VOLUME)	52-1	$4.95
PASSION IN RIO	54-8	$4.95
RAWHIDE LUST	55-6	$4.95
LUSTY LESSONS	31-9	$4.95
FESTIVAL OF VENUS	37-8	$4.95
INTIMATE PLEASURES	38-6	$4.95
TURKISH DELIGHTS	40-8	$4.95
THE KING OF PLEASURE	45-9	$4.95
JADE EAST	60-2	$4.95
A WEEKEND VISIT	59-9	$4.95
RED DOG SALOON	68-8	$4.95
MORE *PLAYGIRL* FANTASIES	69-6	$4.95
NINA FOXTON	70-X	$4.95
HAREM SONG	73-4	$4.95
KATY'S AWAKENING	74-2	$4.95
CELESTE	75-0	$4.95
ANGELA	76-9	$4.95
END OF INNOCENCE	77-7	$4.95
DEMON HEAT	79-3	$4.95
TUTORED IN LUST	78-5	$4.95
DOUBLE NOVEL	86-6	$6.95
LUST	82-3	$4.95
A MASQUERADE READER	84-X	$4.95
THE BOUDOIR	85-8	$4.95
JUDITH BOSTON	87-4	$4.95
SEDUCTIONS	83-1	$4.95
FRAGRANT ABUSES	88-2	$4.95
SCHOOL FOR SIN	89-0	$4.95
CANNIBAL FLOWER	72-6	$4.95
KIDNAP	90-4	$4.95
DEPRAVED ANGELS	92-0	$4.95
ADAM & EVE	93-9	$4.95

Title	Code	Price
THE YELLOW ROOM	96-3	$4.95
AUTOBIOGRAPHY OF A FLEA III	94-7	$4.95
THE SWEETEST FRUIT	95-5	$4.95
THE ICE MAIDEN	3001-6	$4.95
WANDA	3002-4	$4.95
PROFESSIONAL CHARMER	3003-2	$4.95
WAYWARD	3004-0	$4.95
MASTERING MARY SUE	3005-9	$4.95
SLAVE ISLAND	3006-7	$4.95
WILD HEART	3007-5	$4.95
VICE PARK PLACE	3008-3	$4.95
WHITE THIGHS	3009-1	$4.95
THE INSTRUMENTS OF THE PASSION	3010-5	$4.95
THE PRISONER	3011-3	$4.95
OBSESSIONS	3012-1	$4.95
MAN WITH A MAID: The Conclusion	3013-X	$4.95
CAPTIVE MAIDENS	3014-8	$4.95
THE CATALYST	3015-6	$4.95
THE RELUCTANT CAPTIVE	3022-9	$4.95
ALL THE WAY	3023-7	$4.95
CINDERELLA	3024-5	$4.95
THREE WOMEN	3025-3	$4.95
SLAVES OF CAMEROON	3026-1	$4.95
THE VELVET TONGUE	3029-6	$4.95
NAUGHTIER AT NIGHT	3030-X	$4.95
KUNG FU NUNS	3031-8	$4.95
SILK AND STEEL	3032-6	$4.95
THE DISCIPLINE OF ODETTE	3033-4	$4.95
PAULA	3036-9	$4.95
BLUE TANGO	3037-7	$4.95
THE APPLICANT	3038-5	$4.95
THE SECRET RECORD	3039-3	$6.95
PROVINCETOWN SUMMER	3040-7	$4.95
A CRUMBLING FAÇADE	3043-1	$4.95
SABINE	3046-6	$4.95
DARLING • INNOCENCE	3047-4	$4.95
LOVE IN WARTIME	3044-X	$6.95
DREAM CRUISE	3045-8	$4.95
DUKE COSIMO	3052-0	$4.95
STASI SLUT	3050-4	$4.95
CAROUSEL	3051-2	$4.95
MY DARLING DOMINATRIX	3055-5	$6.95
DISTANT LOVE	3056-3	$4.95
PASSAGE & OTHER STORIES	3057-1	$4.95
MASTER OF TIMBERLAND	3059-8	$4.95
GARDEN OF DELIGHT	3058-X	$4.95
TOURNIQUET	3060-1	$6.95
THE COMPLETE EROTIC READER	3063-6	$4.95
EVIL COMPANIONS	3067-9	$6.95
FOR SALE BY OWNER	3064-4	$4.95
MAN WITH A MAID	3065-2	$4.95
BAD HABITS	3068-7	$4.95
MISS HIGH HEELS	3066-0	$4.95
MAN WITH A MAID II	3071-7	$4.95
KATE PERCIVAL	3072-5	$6.95
SANCTUARY	3073-3	$4.95
ILLUSIONS	3074-1	$6.95
COMPLETE *PLAYGIRL* FANTASIES	3075-X	$4.95

ORDERING IS EASY!

MC/VISA orders can be placed by calling our toll-free number

1-800-458-9640

or mail the coupon below to:

**MASQUERADE BOOKS,
801 SECOND AVENUE,
NEW YORK, N.Y. 10017**

BH 068-7

QTY.	TITLE	NO.	PRICE
	SUBTOTAL		
	POSTAGE & HANDLING		
	TOTAL		

Add $1.00 Postage and Handling for tthe first book and 50¢ for each additional book. Outside the U.S. add $2.00 for the first book, $1.00 for each additional book. New York state residents add 8-1/4% sales tax.

NAME _____

ADDRESS _____ **APT. #** _____

CITY _____ **STATE** _____ **ZIP** _____

TEL. ( ) _____

PAYMENT: ❑ CHECK ❑ MONEY ORDER ❑ VISA ❑ MC

CARD NO. _____ **EXP. DATE** _____

PLEASE ALLOW 4-6 WEEKS DELIVERY. NO C.O.D. ORDERS. PLEASE MAKE ALL CHECKS PAYABLE TO MASQUERADE BOOKS. PAYABLE IN U.S. CURRENCY ONLY.